SHERLOCK HOLMES AND THE SOMERSET HUNT

SHERLOCK HOLMES AND THE SOMERSET HUNT

Rosemary Michaud

Ian Henry Publications

© copyright, Rosemary Michaud, 1993

ISBN 0 86025 276 0

Printed by
Ennisfield, Ltd.,
Telfords Yard, 6-8 The Highway, London E1 9BQ
for
Ian Henry Publications, Ltd.,
20 Park Drive, Romford, Essex RM1 4LH

For
JEREMY BRETT
whose voice I hear
whenever Sherlock Holmes speaks

EDITOR'S NOTE

One of the problems of Holmesian research is the way the papers of the late Dr John H Watson have been dispersed over the years. The story now laid before readers dates from the early years of the association between the detective and his 'Boswell', although internal evidence suggests it was written some years later. Where the manuscript has travelled in the intervening years is unclear, but it came to light in a small town in Massachusetts, U.S.A., in the papers of the late Wilbur Footage, a relation by marriage with the Watson family.
It is now presented, with a few corrections to spelling and grammar, in its original form.

RM
1992

THE SUMMONS

It was a crisp morning in the March of 1883 when the prospect of a hot breakfast finally triumphed over the comfort of my warm bed and I descended to take my place at table opposite Sherlock Holmes. My friend and fellow-lodger had clearly been up and about for some time before me, since he was fully dressed and sitting before a plate bearing the remains of ham and buttered eggs, together with a quantity of cigarette stubs. On his face was the abstracted look which normally indicated conversation to be unwelcome, but, to my surprise, he greeted me as if my arrival was precisely the event he desired.

"Another quarter of an hour and I should have come to wake you, Watson. Tell me what you think of this." He tossed a telegram across the table. "Do you think I ought to trouble myself in this matter?"

I was flattered that my opinion should be canvassed, but the contents of the message seemed to make my observations irrelevant.

> Urgently require your presence. A man's life may depend on you. Details on your arrival. Will pay all expenses plus fee. Reply with time you expect to arrive.   Heywood Melrose

"It came reply paid," Holmes explained, "some forty minutes ago. It is from East Quantock, a village in the hills near Taunton. I cannot make up my mind to go."

These were early days in my friend's unique consultancy and, from my point of view, it seemed that neither his reputation nor his bank balance could afford to ignore a paying client with a life and death problem to hand. "How can you refuse?" I asked.

He shrugged. "Am I the militia, to be trotted here and there under orders, without a word of explanation? Whose life is in danger? What sort of danger? He might have spent a few extra pence upon details."

"Do you know this man Melrose? Is he reliable?"

"I assisted him in a matter of insurance fraud a few years ago. He has too little in the way of imagination to deceive himself and is too honest a fellow to be guilty of deceiving me. I may thus conclude that there is indeed a danger or, at least, a convincing appearance of it."

"Then you must go, Holmes!"

"But to the West Country, Watson! Think of the hours of tedium upon the Great Western."

"It is not so very far to go to save a man's life."

"And if I go, I shall have to delay my experiment for several days at the least."

"Your experiment?" I queried.

"Have you forgotten? Ah, well, it has been some time since we discussed it. I have had to wait for the weather to brighten sufficiently for me to collect my specimens. You see, I have been down to the mews only this morning."

He gestured to his work table, where sat some half a dozen jars, each containing a number of very active flies. I now recalled his hypothesis, that the time of death might in certain circumstances be ascertained by the presence of fly eggs and the development of larvae upon the cadaver. My face must have betrayed my distaste for this particular field of scientific endeavour.

"Perhaps, Watson, you would handle this Somerset business while I perform my tests upon the flies."

"I shall certainly go to Taunton, if you will not," I said. "A man of my profession might well be needed there if you refuse to give your help."

The mocking smile faded from his lips and I thought for a moment I had gone too far. Instead, he leapt to his feet. "You are quite right, my friend," said he, striding to the window and throwing it open to the brisk winds, at the same time releasing the imprisoned insects into the air. "There will be flies enough in London upon my return. Now then, it only remains to ask you if you would be willing to join me?"

"Certainly, if you think I may be of use to you."

"I may well require an ally if I am to work so far afield. If nothing else, the journey will pass more quickly with an amiable companion."

§§§

Sherlock Holmes did not suffer unduly from the tedium of railway travel; no sooner were we under way than he curled himself into a corner of the swaying carriage, wrapped himself in his ulster, and fell sound asleep, leaving me to leaf through the newspapers and watch the rural scene that sped past our window. Had the springtime been further advanced the views would have been lovely, but for all that Holmes had found the stable flies buzzing for his jars, the season had yet to burst fully upon us. And yet, despite the barren fields and the stark lines of the leafless trees, there remained the unmistakable signs of that blessed green tranquillity that breathes the very essence of England to native and foreigner alike.

It was midway through the afternoon when a local train that we had caught at Taunton eased into the tiny platform of East Quantock station and we alighted into the fresh country air, untainted by London smoke. The porter, seeing that we were his only two disembarking passengers and that we were two able-bodied men needing no assistance with our scanty baggage, nodded a friendly greeting to us as he headed back into the snug of the ticket office. The train was already chugging away with a rhythmic expulsion of steam as Holmes unlatched the wicket that led from the platform into the village street.

The narrow lane on both sides was lined by half-timbered cottages, marking this as the older part of the village, against which the ruddy brick of the railway station stood uneasily. We looked about for signs of Holmes' insurance man and, seeing a chaise with a handsome grey cob in its traces, we bent our steps towards it. We were still some yards away when a woman of striking beauty leaned from under the hood to hail my friend. "Are you Mr Holmes?"

He bowed briefly, but graciously. "Indeed I am, Miss Melrose."

"You recognised me," she laughed.

"Certainly, though I had not made the connection between your uncle's surname and your own until this moment. This is my good friend, Dr Watson. Watson, surely you recall Miss Jane Melrose from H B Irving's production of *Romeo* at the Lyceum?"

"It is an honour and a pleasure to meet you, Miss Melrose," I gallantly responded.

"You are a doctor!" she exclaimed with considerable enthusiasm.

I was about to explain that I was not now in active practice, when Sherlock Holmes interrupted.

"Dr Watson would be happy to offer his services to your fiancé, would you not, doctor?"

"Oh, I would be most grateful if you could examine him," responded the lady. "Old Dr Farthingale does his best, I'm sure, but a London doctor would be so much more - but, Mr Holmes, how can you know that my fiancé is injured? I cannot believe that my uncle broke his word as to secrecy."

"Not at all. He simply telegraphed that a man's life might be in danger, implying a life other than his own. Upon your left hand, Miss Melrose, I see an engagement ring, which suggests the man to be your fiancé. Your eagerness to consult my friend's advice indicates that he has already suffered some injury. I might make a further deduction that his injury is not serious, or you yourself would not have made the journey to meet us. Instead, you have left your uncle on guard against further peril and come yourself to tell us the facts of the case."

"It is all as you say, Mr Holmes. But come, both of you. There is much to explain before we reach the house."

As we settled into the waiting carriage, I took the opportunity to observe our new acquaintance. The first thing one noticed was her shining light brown hair, dressed to perfection in the latest style, forming a lovely frame for her rich brown eyes and dainty features. Her clothing was subdued in tone and cut, but her natural advantages of figure needed no gaudy dress to augment them. Her confident bearing gave me the impression that she was not quite so young as she appeared to be, but for all I could tell, she might well have been any age between twenty-five and thirty-five. But what gentleman would consider such a question for a moment? I only know that I felt myself quite envious of the man to whom this beautiful woman was betrothed.

When she began to tell her story, it became clear that her beauty was far from being her only attribute. She spoke in the clear, direct manner that comes from a capable intelligence and a determined character.

"Let me explain to you the difficulties of the situation," she began as the brisk trot of the horse's hooves set the wheels turning. "A few weeks ago I became engaged to Mr Andrew Hewitt, the youngest son of

Colonel Laurence Hewitt, the famous soldier."

"The hero of Rashesh?" I interposed.

"That is he. The Hewitt family has long been distinguished. They established their estate in the time of Charles II and their wealth, lands and reputation have increased over the years. The Colonel's exploits have enhanced this reputation and it is said that he should have received recognition long since, but for the fact that his outspoken nature has made him enemies in high places.

"My family - though they are few, save my uncle and some distant cousins - are delighted by my good fortune in marrying the son of such an old and honoured family. The Hewitts, though, are less than pleased by Andrew's choice of an actress to be his wife. Gentlemen, if you know anything of the stage, you will know that my name has never been associated with as much as a hint of scandal. My uncle's generosity has enabled me to avoid many of the unfortunate decisions that a young actress may have to make before she finds success upon the boards, and I earn my living honestly. I like to believe that my talents and my honour speak for themselves. You may well imagine my disappointment and pain on learning that the family I am about to join has no welcome for me. Colonel Hewitt is the most adamant against me and has even gone so far as to tell me to my face that I ought not to marry his son. It is all so very discouraging.

"Please excuse me one moment while I arrange these rugs around me. Why, thank you, Dr Watson. This chaise is rather windy, is it not? There are more rugs under your seats if you too feel the chill."

Holmes smiled without humour. "One would think that the distinguished Hewitts might have provided a closed carriage for you at this time of year."

"Oh, dear, you'll think Andrew's family is worse than it is. No, it isn't that they want me to catch my death, far from that. Andrew says that they don't keep a closed carriage. I'm fortunate that the chaise is in working order. You see, there are no women in the household and the men all prefer to ride horseback wherever they go. This chaise is left from when Andrew's mother was alive. She was liable to become ill if she had to travel in a closed conveyance and therefore she employed either this open-air chaise or else a simple cart for her travels, no matter the weather. I believe she was quite a marvellous lady; whatever suited her will do splendidly for me, too.

"But I have departed from my story, forgive me. My uncle and I came to the family home - Coombehill it is called - at Andrew's request, to try to soften his father's feelings against me by letting him see that I am an ordinary young woman and not an adventuress. Were it not for Andrew's sake, I should have left already. After what happened yesterday, I begin to think that for Andrew's sake it would have been better had I left."

Holmes, who had begun to show some signs of restlessness during Miss Melrose's tale of family discord, now leant forward eagerly, giving the impression that every feature and every nerve were employed to listen.

"I must explain that all the Hewitt family belong to the local hunt," the girl continued, "and they are obsessed with horses and hounds. It is as natural for them to go riding each day as it is for them to eat their meals. So it was that Andrew rode out yesterday with his father and his brothers, David and Ned, although there was no actual meet. My uncle and I are both townees and unaccustomed to the style of riding of which the Hewitts are capable. We stayed at the house and, therefore, I was not present when the mishap occurred, but I can tell you all the details that I have been able to learn from Andrew and his brother Ned.

"They rode slowly at first, but there is a point along the path where the woods open into a broad meadow upon the right hand side. To reach the meadow it is necessary to cross a small stream, running parallel to the pathway. Andrew urged his horse to jump the water. As they landed on the further bank the stirrup gave way and Andrew took a terrible fall. The doctor says he was not seriously injured and will make a complete recovery, but when I think what might have happened to my dear -"

"Miss Melrose," Holmes interrupted, "what is it that makes you presume there was more to this fall than the mere accident of a worn stirrup leather? Did you examine the saddle?"

"I never would have thought to do so. Nor would my Andrew, for that matter. It was my uncle who did. But may I continue the story in order? Otherwise I fear I shall leave out something of importance. When Andrew fell, he lay unconscious at first, so that no one knew how serious his injury might be. His father and Ned remained with him, while his eldest brother rode back to the house to send for Dr Farthingale and to fetch a cart in which to bring Andrew back. Since I wanted to be with Andrew, my uncle and I returned in the cart with David."

"Who drove the cart?"

"Old Pratt, the groom."

"So that Pratt was driving, you and your uncle rode in the cart and David Hewitt rode beside to show the way to the spot?"

The girl nodded.

"And when you reached the meadow, what did you find?"

"I found my poor boy only half sensible, stretched out upon the grass with his head and shoulders cradled in his father's arms."

"Where was the other brother, Ned?"

"He was standing nearby, waving to us to hurry and pointing to the shallowest spot in the stream where the cart could most easily cross."

"Can you recall anything that was said by anyone?"

"Colonel Hewitt's language was such as a lady might not repeat. Suffice to say, there was nothing specific in what he said, until he saw me and told me to keep out of the way."

"Are you saying that he swore angrily, Miss Melrose?"

"Somewhat angrily. He was certainly upset."

"What happened next?"

"Andrew's father and elder brother lifted him into the cart. My uncle helped them, while the groom held the horse steady so the cart should not move. Once Andrew was settled, I climbed into the cart with him, and we immediately started for the house."

"What did brother David do during this time?"

"I did not observe; I was so concerned with the condition of my fiancé."

"Of course. So, the groom drove the cart back with you and the injured man – and y ur uncle?"

"No, the cart was too small. There was no room for

uncle, and therefore he proposed to ride back on Andrew's horse, not knowing that the saddle was damaged. But in going towards Grenadier, he discovered the stirrup upon the ground. He had some thoughts that he might be able to re-attach it, but he could not find the leather strap with which to do so. It was then that Ned approached to warn him against trying to ride Andrew's horse, saying he was far too spirited an animal for an inexperienced man to ride. My uncle told him of the missing stirrup leather, and together they made a brief search for it without success. Then they rode back together on Ned's horse, leading Andrew's horse behind them."

"Can you be absolutely certain that the stirrup leather was removed from the ground?"

"At first, my uncle thought he simply must have missed it. He had not much to do whilst I was with Andrew in the sick room and he felt some curiosity as to what might have been the matter with the stirrup, so he walked back to the scene of the accident and searched again. The stirrup leather was nowhere to be found. He was forced to consider the possibility that someone had removed the leather to conceal the fact that it had been cut or weakened in some way, so as to cause Andrew's fall."

"Which stirrup was it which gave way?"

"The right."

"Ahh, yes. If one were to choose which stirrup to damage, it would be the right, as the left might give way prematurely under the strain of mounting. Why do you suppose someone should wish to harm Andrew Hewitt?"

"I can only think that someone wants to prevent or delay our marriage."

"You will forgive my saying so, Miss Melrose, but surely it would be logical for a member of the Hewitt family to attempt to injure you, rather than their own relation."

"I see that, Mr Holmes, but what other motive could there be for anyone to injure my fiancé?"

"Has he no enemies?"

"None." She shook her head emphatically.

"Can you be sure? Unless I am much mistaken, you have not known him for very long."

"That is true," admitted the lady, with a look of

surprise, "but how do you know it?"

"Well, of course you would have met at least some members of his family before now, had your acquaintance covered a greater span of time. Tell me, have you spoken of your suspicions to anyone else? To your fiancé?"

"Only to him and he refuses to believe that it was anything more than an accident."

"And yet you and your uncle feel otherwise. You seem to be a sensible young woman, Miss Melrose; what is it that you have not yet told us which makes you believe that this might be foul play?"

"It is the sum of many things that has made us wonder, Mr Holmes. Andrew's fall itself... the mystery of the stirrup... the family history..."

"What history is that?"

"This is not the first such accident to befall the Hewitt family. Years ago Andrew's uncle, the Colonel's elder brother, died when his horse fell upon him during a hunt."

"How many years ago was this?"

"Thirty. The year before my Andrew was born."

"Is there more to the family history?" probed Holmes.

"This is difficult to put into words. I could be making more of the family quarrels than is justified, but the fact is that the family have had their troubles ever since the disappearance of the mother, three years ago."

"Disappearance?" Holmes pounced. "Did she leave her husband?"

"No one knows what happened to her. The family is divided in their theories as to her fate. Andrew believes that she is dead. His father says she deserted him."

"Are you saying that she simply vanished? With no word to a soul?"

"Not that the Hewitts have ever heard."

"And no trace of violence?" Holmes mused, "I never heard of this case. Three years ago, you say?"

"Yes, three years last October."

"In this part of Somerset?"

"She was last seen at a neighbour's home, not four miles from here."

"That is certainly remarkable. A household which misplaces its mistress bears some watching the next time something unusual occurs concerning one of the family.

But there is more, I suspect. Hold nothing back, Miss Melrose. I can only help you if I know all that you know."

Holmes' quick eye had discerned a slight hesitation on the part of our hostess, as if she could not make up her mind to tell us the rest of the story. Now in answer to his kindly urging, she appeared to reach a decision, and with trembling hands she drew a folded piece of paper from her reticule and handed it across to him.

"I found this note slipped under the door of my room on my first night at Coombehill."

Holmes was clearly gratified by a sight of the first tangible evidence in the case. The message that I read over his shoulder was brief, unsigned and penned in a decidedly masculine hand:

> I can make it worth your while to end your engagement. If you are interested in my offer, meet me in the summer house at midnight. Bring your uncle if you wish.

Sherlock Holmes studied the paper back and front. "And did you meet this person?" he asked.

Both Miss Melrose and I stared at him in disbelief. As if any respectable woman could even consider keeping such a dubious tryst!

"I did not, Mr Holmes!"

Although I had only just made this lady's acquaintance, I found myself outraged at the thought of her being subjected to this sort of humiliation. "What was your uncle's reaction to this abominable offer?" I enquired.

"I dared not show it to him, doctor. He is a quiet man and slow to anger, but if he knew of this I fear that relations between our families would be broken beyond repair. I thought it better to ignore the note altogether and, by ignoring it, give it the plainest refusal possible."

"Quite right," I applauded.

"Quite," snapped Holmes, betraying his feeling that an opportunity had been lost. Curiosity ranked so far up his scale of values that it was sometimes difficult for him to accept the fact that the lives of other mortals were ruled by more conventional motivation. "May I keep the note?" he asked more gently.

"Please do. But never show it to my uncle."

"You need have no fear of that. Now, Miss Melrose,

tell me everything you did on the day you arrived at East Quantock."

The lady reflected. "We arrived late in the day. I had some business matters to attend to concerning my next play, and I couldn't get away until the middle of the afternoon. Andrew, Uncle Heywood and I all came down on the 3.42 from Paddington. Dixon - he's our driver now - drove us from the station to the house. We just had time to change our clothes for dinner. Oh, that dreadful dinner! My first meeting with the family - all three of them at once - and each of them arrayed against me."

"Was anything said to you that might be construed as a threat?"

"No. Nothing was said to me at all. Andrew tried at first to include me in the conversation, but to tell the truth, I was happy when they all began to talk about the horses and forgot me entirely."

"What did they speak of beside the horses?"

"They asked Andrew about a cousin in London, about the London weather, and if he had sold any paintings."

"Ah, he is an artist."

"Oh, yes, he does marvellous work."

"Was that all there was to the dinner conversation? Nothing that strikes you now as suspicious?"

"No, it was not the words, but the coldness. And their manner towards Andrew is hard to bear. They condescend to him, belittle him. It made me very angry. One would almost think that -" Miss Melrose broke off and put a hand to her mouth.

"Think what? Do continue."

"This is just my impression. I'm sure a policeman would want only facts."

"I am not a policeman, madam," Holmes rejoined stiffly, "and I am very much interested in your impressions. Your particular occupation makes your observations of double value, since you have been trained to see and express the subtleties of human behaviour."

"It seems to me, since you mention my profession, that, although the stated objection to my marrying into the family concerns this out-dated impression of an actress' virtue, that the real objection goes deeper. I believe that had Andrew chosen a princess for his wife, the family would nevertheless have some complaint."

I had to admit to some confusion. "Do you mean that no woman is good enough for Colonel Hewitt's son?"

"No, I mean that Andrew's position in the family is such that they mistrust or disapprove of everything he does. No woman that he chose could be suitable, simply because he has chosen her."

Holmes pursed his lips thoughtfully. "Why is that?"

"You do not expect me to say a word against the man I love?"

"Ah, well, is your love blind or simply mute? Please, Miss Melrose, explain what you can for us. It is certainly clear that Andrew Hewitt has chosen a help-meet very wisely; therefore it can do no harm for you to tell us what his family see as his failings."

"Should he have any failings that are worth noting, I suppose the worst of them is that he sometimes speaks carelessly, sometimes out of a merry humour, and sometimes to avoid difficult situations. You see, he is so very sweet and kind-hearted that he tries to draw back from unpleasantness if he can. He is quite talkative by nature. Oh, he has the most beautiful voice! You cannot imagine what a pleasure it is just to listen to him! However, anyone who takes every word he says seriously at face value may find himself confused or maybe annoyed. I always tell him he could have been an actor himself, so you see, I could hardly find fault with that. But I suppose that a colonel lately in Her Majesty's cavalry might see it in a different light. Of course, it almost goes without saying that his father disapproves of his choice of profession."

"And after that difficult supper, what did you do?"

"Andrew and I - and Uncle Heywood, of course, - went to his mother's old room to look at some family photographs and the like."

"Did anything strike you about what you saw?"

"I especially loved Mrs Hewitt's drawings. Her sketchbooks are filled with family scenes and it was fascinating to see her perspective of Andrew as a boy. It's clear that he was her favourite and her drawings show that love."

"Did anyone else in the family know you saw the sketchbooks and the rest?"

"Why, yes. Ned Hewitt asked his brother how he

planned to spend the evening, and Andrew told him."

"Returning to the dinner conversation: can you recall who it was who asked if your fiancé had sold any work?"

"It was his father."

"Had he sold any? Does he earn his living by his painting?"

"He has sold a few and he earns a pittance, but in the main he is supported by his income from the family trust."

"Has there been any threat to cut him off from that income, in view of your impending marriage?"

"Not to my knowledge."

"How considerable is the Hewitt income?"

"There is the estate, with its tenant farmers and, I believe, a large sum of investments. You must realise that I would not enquire as to the value; I would not wish it to seem that I have designs on any portion of it."

"Of course not. Although," Holmes mused, patting the coat pocket into which he had placed the mysterious note, "it may be that someone thinks you do. It must have been upon his elder brother's death that the colonel took possession of the family inheritance?"

"I believe so."

"Your fiancé is the youngest of the colonel's sons?"

"David is the eldest, Ned - Edward - is nine years Andrew's senior and is the closest to him in affection."

"Has he a profession?"

"He has studied law and is a solicitor with offices in Taunton. Andrew says that he has some political aspirations."

"Has the colonel been in ill health recently, do you know?"

"Far from it, Mr Holmes. He is as hale as many a man half his age."

"Indeed. Tell me about your acquaintance with your fiancé. When and where did you meet?"

Our pretty companion blushed and laughed. "Really, Mr Holmes," she protested.

"Miss Melrose," said my friend, impervious to her embarrassment, "I cannot say what the source of the danger to your fiancé might be, and there is no telling what piece of information may be critical to finding it out."

"You will think us mad, I am afraid," confessed the

girl. "We fell in love at first sight when he saw me upon the stage and my eyes chanced on him where he sat in the audience. He arranged that we should meet and we found our eyes had not deceived us and that truly we were meant to share the rest of our lives, the one with the other."

"How long has Andrew lived in London, where I presume he does his painting?"

"Three years, I think. Not much more, at any rate."

"And you met?"

"This past December."

"Does none of your fiancé's family approve of his marriage?"

"Ned seems prepared to accept it."

"Very good, Miss Melrose. Now - who at Coombehill knows we are coming?"

"Everyone knows, but they believe that Andrew has invited a cousin of mine for the hunt. I did not know there would be two of you."

"We will get around that problem easily enough. I think that it would be better if our actual purpose remained a secret, if for no other reason than that your fears are as yet of an indefinite form."

"You mean to say that I may well be mistaken. I fully admit it, gentlemen. If the family resent my presence now, imagine how they would feel if they knew I suspected one of them of - of whatever it is that has happened."

"I understand your quandary. Well, though the suggestion flatters him in the extreme, I believe that Dr Watson would be the more credible in the role of your cousin. Have you any objections to that, Miss Melrose?"

"None at all," said she with a friendly smile in my direction. "And what about you, Mr Holmes?"

"Let us say that I am an acquaintance of yours from the theatre - a theatrical manager, say - with an interest in art. As a friend of Watson's, I invited myself along with him to strike up a friendship with your fiancé and perhaps to invest a little sum in his work. You will remain as nearly yourself as possible, Watson; Miss Melrose and I will do all the acting that is required."

I muttered that I was pleased to hear it, although secretly it rankled that my friend had felt it necessary to display his lack of confidence in my abilities while our client was present.

"Good," said Holmes. "Now then, perhaps you and Miss Melrose ought to use the remainder of our journey to share any information that may be of use to you in your roles as cousins."

Holmes turned his face towards the side of the chaise, as a man might were he in need of fresh air – though it was hardly necessary to lean out to catch the breeze. From the set of his jaw and the nervous motions of his fingers, I knew that his active mind had already begun to sort through the story we had heard, forming those subtle and intuitive links between facts that would lead him to the centre of the maze.

I feared that his distant manner would be upsetting to our companion, but she, after regarding him for a long moment with some curiosity, turned to me brightly and began to sketch in some important facts of her own and her family's history. I responded in kind, and so we passed the following fifteen minutes.

In less time than I should have wished our carriage turned into a long drive that curved up the side of a long hill, through a grove of ancient elms. Near the crest of the hill the trees opened out on to a flat lawn that stretched the final hundred yards or so to the eastern face of a great house. In later spring, the expanse of grass would have cheered the prospect somewhat, but at this time of year, and under grey skies, the yellowed lawn and the absence of leaves on the trees gave the place a bleak and blasted look.

Although built since the days when gunpowder had made stone fortresses obsolete, the house seemed to retain a hint of that louring architectural style. One could easily picture a troop of mounted men issuing from the main entrance. The numerous tall windows might have relieved the imposing face of the building had they not been arranged in such a way that they called to mind the set order of marching ranks of soldiers. The only touch of whimsy in the entire façade was a cupola perched in the very centre of the high roof, but I looked long and hard to catch sight of a siege gun or the glint of a sentry's rifle there. Such was the immediate impression created by Coombehill: I speculated as to what it must have been like to grow up within these rigid walls.

Nothing on the outside prepared us for the sight that met the eye inside. We found ourselves stepping into one of the most spectacular entrance halls I have ever seen. Before us stretched a parquet floor, polished to shimmering brightness reflecting the crystal chandelier that hung a full storey above our heads. Before us, twin staircases wound their way to the first floor and, as we mounted that on the left hand side on our way to the sick--room, I half expected to meet some brightly-gowned ladies descending to take their place in the hall. A glance at Holmes showed me that he too had noted the dramatic contrast.

What sort of people would we find here?

THE ACCIDENT

When Miss Jane Melrose had described the events leading up to her engagement I had found myself wondering what sort of man might be capable of turning the head of such a lovely and gifted woman - and from his seat in a darkened theatre, at that. As we entered the sick room my question was answered. Even in his dishevelled condition as an invalid, Mr Andrew Hewitt was a strikingly handsome man. His face bore the accepted features of aristocracy: high cheekbones, a sensitive mouth and a slightly curved, patrician nose. He wore his dark brown hair a trifle over-long, as if to accentuate its boyish unruliness. Had I not already known from Miss Melrose that he was only two years my junior, I should have put him as barely past his majority, so fresh and unmarred were his features. These observations on his appearance were secondary, however, after the first impression of his remarkable pair of deep-set jade-green eyes, glimmering below his dark brows.

"Jane! he cried, extending his hand to her and flashing an angelic smile. "And you gentlemen are the detectives from London? How good of you both to come."

Miss Melrose presented us formally both to her fiancè and her uncle, who had been sitting so quietly in the corner that I had quite overlooked him. Now the insurance man got to his feet and shook hands with my friend.

"I cannot sufficiently express my thanks to you for coming, Mr Holmes." Then, with a guarded look in my direction, he commented, "You've taken on an assistant since we last met?"

"Dr Watson is my occasional assistant and constant friend. His trustworthiness is beyond all question."

Melrose's manner brightened at once and he pumped my hand with enthusiasm. "If you are beyond Mr Holmes' style of questions, doctor, you are trustworthy indeed!"

I scarcely had a chance to acknowledge this statement, for Holmes, eager to begin and ever impatient with the niceties of social intercourse, had already turned to the young man. "Miss Melrose has told us of your misfortune, but I am most interested to hear it from your point of view, Mr Hewitt."

"I won't be of much help, I'm afraid," said the injured man with a light laugh. He had a light tenor voice and spoke with the careless attitude of one accustomed all his life to winning others to his side with charm and a pleasing appearance. Indeed, there was something appealing about him - a childish enthusiasm that most men have found it necessary to discard long before their thirtieth birthday.

His manner seemed to nettle Holmes in some way, however. "How do you explain the missing stirrup leather?" asked the detective curtly.

"I imagine it's simply lost."

"That is a possibility, course," replied Holmes. "Tell me what happened yesterday."

"Well, I jumped Grenadier over the stream, my off stirrup gave way, and down I went."

Holmes betrayed his impatience with a click of the tongue. "A bit more detail would be helpful, Mr Hewitt."

"I am the last man on earth who could give you details. Before I fell, I suspected nothing. After I fell, I remember nothing. I struck my shoulder and my head, or so I am given to understand. My only recollections are hazy in the extreme."

"Let us pass over that for the time being, then. When had you last visited your family here, prior to bringing Miss Melrose?"

"I was here for two weeks at the New Year."

"And did you go riding?"

"A little, but the weather was not favourable for much of my visit."

"But there were no accidents at that time?"

Andrew Hewitt shook his head - and winced from a twinge from his injuries.

Holmes persisted. "You rode the same horse?"

"Yes. Grenadier is my own horse, though he stays here while I am in London. I only ride him when I visit."

"As of your last visit you were not engaged to Miss Melrose?"

"Well - that depends on how one uses the word. We were already certain that we would marry, but we had not discussed it in so many words, if you follow my meaning."

"Had you told anyone else of your plans?"

"Our friends in London knew. I hesitated to tell my family at first. I knew how my father would react, you see. Still, Ned guessed that something was on my mind, and I did confess to him that I had fallen in love."

During this exchange Holmes had been examining the room with critical eye, staring with particular interest at a painting on the wall by the bed-head. It was a night scene of a tree-lined country lane covered in snow, as viewed from inside a glistening window. From a distance it seemed a pretty enough picture. However, when I looked closely, it seemed somehow indistinct, with an imbalance in the perspective and a bizarre approach to colour that made an unsettling impression on me. Holmes seemed more favourably struck by it, though, and he turned to Hewitt with a new note of respect in his voice.

"This is your work?"

The artist laughed. "It is. You must not seem so surprised that I have some abilities, Mr Holmes. It's what God gave me instead of brains. I freely admit I have few of those."

"I should not have been surprised at your abilities had Miss Melrose told me that she was engaged to Mr Andrew Fitzhenry, as well as to Mr Andrew Hewitt."

"I have signed my mother's maiden name to my work for years, to protect the proud name of Hewitt from the contamination of my vocation. Bless you for having heard of me, Mr Holmes."

"I saw your work in the Baxter Galleries a few months past and I was struck by the resemblance of your style to that of Armand Guillaumin."

"I have been accused of flattering him by imitation."

"Your own style will assert itself in time. Your family need not be ashamed of work such as yours."

"You sound just the man to talk to my father!"

"First we must ensure that your career will not be cut short. It is fortunate that you fell to the right side or you might have found yourself unable to paint."

"Aren't you the clever one! Yes, I am left-handed. Uncle Melrose, where did you find a detective with an artist's eye? Mr Holmes, perhaps you would like to see some of my other efforts while you are here."

"That would give me great pleasure, but, I repeat, my first consideration is for your safety."

"I cannot believe that there is anyone in this world who wishes me harm. The accident was my own fault; I ought to have checked the stirrup leathers before ever I mounted. My father always taught us to check our tack before a ride. But anyone can tell you, I always think of care and prudence when it's too late."

"There, you see, Mr Hewitt, anyone familiar with your nature and your habits could lay their plans with your carelessness in mind."

"Oh, I see what you mean. But what reason would anyone have for causing me to fall?"

"Can you think of any reason? A family quarrel, perhaps?"

"Family, Mr Holmes?" For an instant the sparkling green eyes flashed away from us, as if an unformed fear had passed through his mind. It was a small gesture, but I saw that Holmes had observed it too. "Do you suspect my family?"

"In the early stages of an investigation I try to keep my mind as open as possible. Various members of your family were there when you fell; in fact, they are the only people with an opportunity to have removed the damaged stirrup leather from the scene of the accident."

"So your idea is that whoever removed it must have damaged it in the first place?"

"Not necessarily - though probably."

"I suspect that wretched leather is out there somewhere, lying under a bunch of leaves, and this whole business is nothing but the result of bad luck and a lack of precaution on my part."

"That is possible," responded Holmes. "It would be as well if Watson and I went out to look for ourselves before we reach any false conclusions. In the mean time, it can do no harm for you to avoid being alone. Remain in the company either of Miss Melrose or her uncle at all times. Oh, and Miss Melrose, please explain to Mr Hewitt and your uncle that Watson here is your cousin and all the rest of our story. Now, Mr Hewitt, is the location of your tumble an easy spot to find or should we require a guide?"

Andrew Hewitt gave us directions and asked Holmes to ring for a manservant who could saddle us a couple of horses. As Holmes leaned across to the bell-pull, he picked up a beautifully engraved silver pocket-knife. "Were you carrying this knife when you fell?"

Hewitt replied in the affirmative and asked why Holmes enquired as the detective slipped it into his pocket.

"Should anyone ask where we are going," replied Holmes, "you can tell them that we are looking for your knife. Do you understand?"

Hewitt's brow cleared. "I see! Anyone would think that I had dropped it when I fell."

Holmes inclined his head, smiling. "And now, if I might presume upon your courtesy - I should very much like to ride the same horse you were riding when you fell."

"Mr Holmes, you don't know what you are asking. I suspect that Grenadier would be too much for you."

"Is he simply high in spirits - or has he particular failings?"

"He is high-spirited enough, but he isn't ridden often these days. He's always a bit of a handful at the start and I truly doubt that any London man could handle him."

Holmes rejoined, "I was not always a Londoner."

§§§

The horse provided for me appeared tractable enough, but the towering red roan led out for Holmes danced at the groom's hand as if the bridle reins were his only tether to the earth. My friend carefully checked the saddle, made a small adjustment to the stirrups, then, disdaining the mounting block nearby, gathered the reins into his hands and stepped nimbly up on to the great horse's back.

For a moment Grenadier stood perfectly still, eyes rolled back and nostrils quivering, as if he could scarcely believe that a stranger had had the temerity to mount him. Then, all at once, his front hooves left the ground and he rose until his back was nearly perpendicular. Just as I feared that both horse and man would go over backwards, the flailing hooves returned to ground with a jolt. Now frustrated more than ever that he had not dislodged his burden, he began to prance in a circle, tossing his head the while, as if the bit between his teeth was unbearably galling. Through it all, Holmes kept his seat firm and his hands steady, upon his face an expression of eagerness, as one relishing a challenge. With supreme confidence and skill he suffered the animal's opening tantrum and slowly brought him to hand. In five minutes more we were riding side by side along the path as sedately as one could wish.

"Holmes," I said, "you never cease to amaze me with the range of your accomplishments. I never supposed you were such a horseman."

My friend waved my remark away with a gesture, but I could see that he was not displeased. "Do you understand why I wish to ride this horse?" he asked.

I replied that I assumed that the horse would have the same saddle and enquired what Holmes had deduced from the stirrup.

"The right stirrup leather is new, while the left has seen more wear. It would be a fool who would attempt precisely the same trick twice running. The point is that the saddle is not very old or worn and therefore not likely to give way without a little help. What do you think of our friend, the artist?"

"He seems decidedly off-hand about this matter. I wonder that he allowed Miss Melrose and her uncle to send for you at all."

"Were you engaged to wed Miss Jane Melrose, I feel certain that you would be equally malleable in indulging her whims."

I allowed this suggestion, "Did you truly admire Hewitt's paintings?" I further enquired, "or were you simply gaining his confidence?"

"Watson, you surprise me. When have you ever known me to flatter a man with unmerited praise? The fellow has a good eye and the hand to express what he sees. I take it that you do not appreciate his work?"

I shook my head and Holmes laughed, at the same time announcing that we had found the spot and demanding that I hold Grenadier's head while he dismounted.

For half an hour he searched the banks of the stream, the surrounding grassy areas, the shallow waters, the rocks, the shrubs. Then, with a shrug of his shoulders, he returned to stroke the nose of the great red horse, who was now showing every sign of accepting him as an acquaintance.

"How very fortunate that Hewitt chose this spot for his first jump," Holmes commented. "One could as easily gallop through the stream as leap it and the impact of his fall was certainly less than had he chosen a higher or a broader obstacle for his first try."

I remarked that the soft bank of the stream had made for an easier fall and asked what other conclusions Holmes might have reached.

"Wait here a moment," he commanded, mounting Grenadier and crossing the stream back towards the main track. Then, kicking his feet out of the stirrups, he urged the horse on again towards where I stood. Man and beast sailed easily over the narrow obstacle, but, without the support of the stirrups, Holmes came tumbling out of the saddle the moment the horse's hooves made renewed contact with the earth. Holmes rolled to a stop yards from me, but before I could reach him, he had pulled himself to a sitting position and waved me back with a laugh.

"You're not hurt?" I asked, just to be certain.

"Not at all," said he. "I'm a trifle muddy, but I shall survive it, I'm sure. Be a good fellow and catch the horse, will you?"

When we had both remounted, Holmes saw fit to explain his actions to me. "You see, Watson, a competent horseman could have ridden to this point without the stirrup in place at all, since he would not need the off stirrup in order to mount."

"Are you suggesting that Hewitt staged the mishap?"

"I am saying that it is possible he did."

"But how is it that the stirrup iron was found at the scene of the fall?"

"Dropped from his pocket as the horse jumped."

"We don't know that he is as skilled a rider as you."

"I think it likely that he is more skilled than I. Painter or not, he is the son of a cavalryman, Watson, and he has ridden to hounds all his life. He may not be quite so skilled in acrobatics, however."

"And therefore his injuries, you mean?"

"Yes, they seem to be genuine enough, though I should like your professional opinion in that regard when we return to the Hall."

"But what could be his motive for making it appear that someone had tried to injure him? After all, he accuses no-one."

"We must not eliminate a possible explanation simply because we do not know the motive behind it."

"But he doesn't give the impression of being a clever schemer, does he?"

"Does he not?" enquired my friend with raised eyebrows.

"You seem to have taken a dislike to him. That isn't like you, Holmes."

"I mistrust a man who boasts of his own stupidity. And I cannot quite believe in his luck at having fallen here, when there were more likely hurdles for him only a few yards away. Look, across the meadow."

I followed the direction of Holmes' gaze and saw what he meant: the grassy meadow sloping gently to our right was separated from a small orchard by a low hedgerow. What could be more natural than for a hearty young horseman to ride at full gallop across the open plain and try the hedgerow in a showy leap?

I was interrupted in my speculations by another rider coming along the path behind us. "Gentlemen," he hailed us, "my brother said I should find you here. My name is Edward Hewitt. You must be Miss Melrose's cousin."

The man offering his hand to me resembled his brother vaguely, but was fairer in colouring than Andrew, and any comparison of their features was obscured by a moustache which dominated the newcomer's thin face. His address to us was correct, but cool, not unlike that which a barrister might employ with his opponent in a courtroom.

"Dr John Watson," I responded, clasping his hand. "This is my friend, Sherlock Holmes."

"I hope you will both excuse my brother's thoughtlessness in sending you out to search for his belongings before you have rested from your journey. I can't think why he did not mention to me that he had lost the knife. We could have sent one of the stable lads out to search, rather than house guests." His words were perfectly proper, but suspicion glinted unmistakably from his hard, blue eyes.

Holmes smiled past the piercing look. "Your brother happened to mention the loss of his knife and Dr Watson and I offered to find it for him. There was no thoughtlessness on his part. We insisted on performing the service and, I am happy to say, we found the knife." So saying he drew the article from his pocket. He had contrived to smear the handle with black mud from the stream-bank, so it looked for all the world as if he had only just taken it from the ground.

"I found it here," he continued, pointing to a spot near the track where the cart had crossed the water. Sure enough, there was a small indentation in the soil, exactly the shape of the pocket-knife. I could hardly credit that it had not lain there for these two days.

"You must have sharp eyes to have seen it, half-buried as it was," said the barrister. "None of us noticed it."

"It is unlikely you would have seen it unless you were looking for it. And, of course, you were occupied with caring for your brother."

"Indeed. He gave us quite a fright. By the way, since you have made a search of the ground, I don't suppose you happened across the broken stirrup leather from my brother's saddle. I don't know if Mr Melrose told you that we could not find it here."

"How very odd. We saw no leather here, did we, Watson? Now you mention it Melrose did say something about not being able to fix the saddle. It's just as well for him, I suppose. I can't picture him astride this creature."

"You seem to have had a spot of trouble yourself," Hewitt remarked, pointing to Holmes' soiled jacket and trousers.

"Grenadier seems to suffer from too much leisure. Will you ride back with us, Mr Hewitt?"

"I regret I have other business which I cannot neglect. I shall see you gentlemen at supper then." His gloved hand had scarcely tipped the brim of his cap before he wheeled his horse and cantered back as he had come.

"I wonder why he followed us here," mused Holmes as we watched him depart. "To see whether we had found the stirrup leather perhaps; which could be taken to imply he does not himself know where it is. He must be aware Melrose is troubled by its disappearance and perhaps he wished to gauge the extent of our suspicions. Did you see his eyes, Watson? There is no lack of intelligence in that member of the Hewitt family. I would give much to follow him, but I dare not show our hand so early in the game."

Edward Hewitt had not returned home, according to the groom who took charge of the horses. Holmes looked thoughtful as we trod the path from the stable to the house.

"Let us look in on the patient once more, shall we, doctor?" suggested the detective. "We need a great deal more information if we are to make any sense of this matter."

THE PATIENT

Andrew Hewitt was with Miss Melrose when we knocked and entered. "Well," said he, "you have obviously survived your introduction to Grenadier. How do you like him?"

"Your brother asked the same question."

"You've met Ned, then. I hope he was civil to you. He was awfully cross when he left us, wasn't he, Jane? He saw you riding off on my horse, you see, and he came storming up here to be sure that I knew of it. I told him about the knife, just as you said. What did he say to you?"

"Very little. Is he always so much on his guard when meeting friends of yours?"

"Don't mind Ned. He still thinks he has to protect his little brother from the wicked world. I apologise for him."

Holmes smiled. "That is not necessary. But do you not think it strange that he should follow us to find out what we were doing?"

"Strange? Mr Holmes, let me make one thing quite clear. It is ridiculous to harbour suspicion about any member of my family, but of all of them, Ned is the last - positively the last - who would ever do me any harm. It's simply impossible and you will only waste your time if you try to cast a slur on him. Were I in trouble, day or night, I would call on Ned for help. This whole idea of detectives is absurd, Jane, with all respect to your uncle. We ought to have simply confided your fears to my brother and the whole business would be settled by now. By God, what a headache you've given me with all this suspicion and subterfuge. Now, Jane, don't cry, please don't. Oh, Jane, I'm a brute, don't cry."

I shuffled my feet in embarrassment and signed to Holmes that it would be polite for us to leave, but Miss Melrose threw out her hand to arrest us. "No, please stay a moment. Don't let my tears scare you away." She turned back to her fiancé. "Andrew, my dearest, I know how unthinkable it must be to you that anyone you love could do you any harm, but here you are - injured - and the cause is still a mystery. Don't you see that you are so precious to me that I must do anything and suspect anyone until I have made certain that you are in no danger?"

The invalid tried to wave her eloquence down, but Miss Melrose was not to be silenced.

"It might have been an accident or a coincidence. I know that it may well be so, but Mr Holmes is said to be the cleverest detective in England and he will be able to find out once and for all what the explanation is. Then you may think what you will of me: that I am a foolish woman or a wise one – or just someone who loves you beyond all reason or propriety."

For a long moment, the lovers lost all awareness of our standing there and, with clasped hands and ardent eyes, they spoke to each other in that language which goes beyond all words. Holmes, unmoved by the tender scene, broke the spell by clearing his throat.

"You will excuse, me, I am sure," said my friend, "but am I to understand that my services are no longer required? Or are they?"

"They are," Hewitt spoke decisively. "They very much are, Mr Holmes. Did you find the stirrup leather?"

"It was not there. And I am bound to say that its absence means that there is every reason to suspect foul play in this matter. As to where the blame may lie, It is too soon to venture an answer. I would prefer that you confide in no member of your family, Mr Hewitt, not because I believe any one of them to be guilty, but because any knowledge of my purpose here might inadvertently warn the truly guilty party and put him on his guard. Do you understand?"

The patient grunted his affirmation.

"And now I believe that the good doctor here ought to keep his promise to Miss Melrose and offer his expert medical opinion on your physical condition."

Hewitt reluctantly submitted to this suggestion and Holmes guided Miss Melrose to the door. I supposed that he too would leave the room to give my patient privacy, but to my surprise he remained behind and hovered about, while I made the best examination I could with the limited tools I had brought with me.

Hewitt's heartbeat was normal and his lungs clear and sound. He had suffered a deep bruise on the point of his right shoulder, but there appeared to be no lasting damage from his recent fall. An older injury caused me concern, however: along the back of his head, covered by his thick dark hair, I found a two inch silvery scar such as might be left by a sharp blow that had split the scalp open. "That must have been a nasty, bloody thing when it happened," I commented.

Hewitt laughed. "So I'm told it was."

Holmes peered to take a look for himself. "How did it happen?"

"Another accident. Good heavens, how you both stare at me! You make me feel like a museum display. And here you have one of Somerset's milder curiosities. The blow to this young gentleman's skull may explain the mystery of his continuous, idle chatter."

I was amused by this banter and laughed with Hewitt. We made, after all, a quaint group with Holmes and I standing and pointing at the poor fellow's cranium. Holmes was not in the mood for badinage. "What sort of accident?" he demanded.

"A riding accident - what else? I seem to have a knack for falling head-foremost, don't I? Luckily I have nothing but cotton wool between my ears. A man with any brains would have had them all addled by now, but it's nothing to me, you see."

"You're a lucky fellow to be able to smile about either fall, you know," I told him.

"I know," replied Hewitt. "May Jane come back now?"

"Not yet," said Sherlock Holmes. "I have a few questions I would like to ask you in private."

"I don't have any secrets from her," objected our client.

"I believe," said Holmes, "that you have told Miss Melrose a great deal about your relations with your father and brothers - much more than she would reveal to us?"

"Must you hear all the unhappy details?" asked the patient with a wry smile.

"Possibly not all, but I must have some degree of background information to guide me. I try not to let my imagination run away with me, Mr Hewitt, but it is so much easier to keep it in check when I have solid facts to savour. Please tell me about you and your father."

"What can I say? My father has never understood me; he is simply not capable of so doing. All my life he has wanted me to be a soldier, you know. You will probably hear him allude to it at least once during your stay: I would be willing to lay money on it that you will."

"Your brothers are not soldiers," I pointed out. "Why were you destined to be a soldier and not they?"

"He wanted them to be soldiers too, of course, only I'm the last - his last chance. He thinks that being a soldier would be the cure for all my faults. And so it would, I agree, because it would be the death of me, don't you see? My father still has hopes that I'll turn out all right, but since I've turned out already and I'm not the least like his conception of a proper son, I imagine we'll be hitting our heads together until they bury one of us. You needn't look at me in that way, Mr Holmes; there isn't the least possibility that it was my father who tampered with my saddle. Even should he wish to hurt me - which he does not - it would not be like him to sneak around planting booby-traps. When my father wants me dead, he'll walk straight up to me and put his hands round my throat!"

"Has he ever done so?" queried Holmes mildly.

"Of course not," retorted Andrew Hewitt.

"When did you move away from the family home?" probed my friend.

"I went to public school when I was a lad - and I was expected to go on to university, but I didn't! Instead, I went to study art in Paris." The young painter laughed. "If my father was ever going to kill me, that would have been the time. When he saw me off, he assumed I was going to Cambridge, but I chose a different route. He might well have throttled me, but I was in Paris by the time he found out what I'd done."

"But you did come back here from time to time?"

"So long as my mother was here, I would always have come back. When she was gone I packed up for London permanently, though I make a point to come back for some of the holidays and as much as I can during the hunting season."

"Do you see any prospect of reconciling your family to your marriage?" asked Holmes.

"They'll all come round in the end. I had hoped that, once they met her, they would see how sweet she is, how unlike what they might have imagined her to be. But wait a year, until we can show my father a beautiful grandchild: all his opposition will melt away."

"It is fortunate that your father has not taken steps to curtail your income as a means of bending you to his will," commented Holmes.

"He can't curtail it. My money is my own, thanks to my mother's foresight. When we were small boys, you see, she persuaded my father to establish irrevocable trusts with some of the money she brought to the marriage, so that Ned and I should never find ourselves in the precarious position so often occupied by younger sons. I am sure that my father has regretted many times that he acceded to her request, at least in my case. Once I reached majority I became - in money terms certainly - independent of his will."

"I assume that, after your marriage, your wife would inherit your estate. But until then, who is your next-of-kin and how large is the trust?"

"Obviously," muttered Hewitt crossly, "as things were arranged, my money would all revert to father. As far as the money goes, I draw an income of about £500 a year from the interest or dividends or whatever - but Ned handles all that sort of thing."

Holmes raised his eyebrows. "A handsome allowance for a younger son. The principal must be quite a substantial sum. The wonder is that your mother ever got your father to consent to diverting it away from the estate."

"But you see, my father was himself a younger son. Until he married into my mother's wealth he was obliged to apply to his father - and later to Uncle Andrew - to purchase his commission and keep up his standing among the officers of the regiment. My mother proposed our trusts not long after father became master of this house and while the memory of his leaner days and lowly position were still fresh."

Sherlock Holmes regarded the artist quizzically saying, "Your uncle's accident brought your father a fortune in his own right. That was a piece of luck for him."

Andrew Hewitt stiffened his back and looked Holmes in the eye. "You can lay the blame for Uncle Andrew's death only on Uncle Andrew. Well, possibly you could accuse the horse of not making the jump, but he was the one who decided to try for the double fence near Kirksey's Farm, and died when they both fell, the horse on top. My uncle was in plain sight of two other riders, who were wiser than to attempt the feat themselves. And for your further information, my father was in India with his regiment when the accident happened."

"And your brothers?"

"They were with my mother in London. She always stayed with her own people when my father was away. But it was thirty years ago, Mr Holmes. Even clever brother Ned would have had all he could do to plan a murder when he was barely eight years old. David wasn't quite ten."

Holmes persisted. "What about Pratt, the old groom? Where was he?"

"With my father. My uncle didn't need any help to go to an early grave, believe me. He was always a roisterer and a dare-devil, always taking chances, drinking too much. I wish I'd known him."

Holmes abandoned that line of enquiry and leaned towards Andrew Hewitt. "Your mother's disappearance was a matter never satisfactorily explained, was it?"

Hewitt bent forward and drew his knees up to his chin. "No," said he, his voice muffled into the bedclothes.

"Tell me what you know about it."

"Mr Holmes, please, I would really rather not. It cannot have any bearing on my own accident." Hewitt glanced at me, asking softly, "Can it?"

"Who can say," I replied. "You would do best to think of my friend as you might a specialist in medicine, to whom you would confide all possible information about your problem, regardless of how unrelated it might seem to your main complaint."

Our client ran his hand through his already-tousled hair. "What do you want to know?"

Holmes slid his chair closer to the bedside. "Tell me the circumstances surrounding her disappearance. Begin with the exact date."

"It was the twenty-first of October, 1879. A Tuesday. We know that she left our neighbour's house, Primrose Hill - the Dudleys lived there in those days - and started for home. Mrs Dudley was sick and my mother was visiting her. That's the sort of person my mother was, you see, the kindest and most generous soul who ever lived. Anyway, she never arrived home. When she was overdue and had sent no word Ned and I rode out to look for her. We found her cart overturned on the road only a little more than a mile from here. There was no sign of my mother. Her driver was unconscious beside the cart and he died that night without regaining his senses."

"Did he die of injuries received when the cart overturned? Did anyone look for signs of other violence?"

"I suppose had there been any signs, Dr Farthingale would have told us. I presume that there were none beyond those he got when he was thrown from the cart."

"Had he been driving at an excessive speed?"

"How could anyone know that?" asked Andrew Hewitt.

"By the hoof prints of the horse, for one thing. Was this matter looked into by the police?"

"Our local inspector enquired. There was a half-empty bottle of wine near the wreck, so it was a good bet that Collins had been drinking."

"It surprises me that your father would keep a man who was fond of the bottle in his service."

"My mother felt sorry for Collins and his family. She thought that steady work would give him confidence and make a better man of him. He seemed to make some improvement, but still he always carried a bottle - for warmth, he said."

Holmes accepted this explanation. "What do you think happened to your mother?"

"I think some stranger waylaid and killed her. Someone she encountered by some awful mischance. Collins was too confused by drink or too cowardly to help her, and he drove off, perhaps with the idea of getting help."

"No one has heard from your mother since that night?" Hewitt shook his head and Holmes pursued the subject. "Had your mother any enemies?"

"Good heavens, no. There wasn't a soul in the West Country who could have wished her any harm. That is why I contend it must have been a stranger."

"Was your parents' marriage happy?"

I expected an indignant response from our client, but his reaction was that of an injured man, not an angry one.

"Why should you ask me such a question, Mr Holmes? My father did not kill my mother. You haven't even met my father. Do you realise that he provided a life income for Collins' widow and children? I consider that a rather stunning gesture of Christian charity, under the circumstances. His whole character revolves around his soldier's code of honour: such a man does not murder his life's partner." Hewitt hesitated, braced his shoulders and continued, "My parents loved each other very much, but they were unhappy together, if you can understand how that may be."

I was somewhat baffled by this statement, but Holmes nodded encouragingly and appeared to change the subject. "Miss Melrose says that your father believes that your mother is not dead, but has simply run away."

"It's that damned note he found: a piece of garbage if you ask me," declared Hewitt.

Holmes raised his eyebrows in enquiry.

Hewitt went on, "The day my mother disappeared my father found a note addressed to her, which seemed to arrange an assignation for that night at the *Red Lion* in Fenny Burton. But it proved itself false, as father went to the pub and waited till well past the time the meeting was to have taken place. Neither my mother nor anyone else appeared."

I felt that a little more light should be set on this incident and asked Hewitt his opinion as to why the note should have been sent at all, but, beyond suggesting that an unknown was trying to tarnish his mother's name, he had no theory.

Holmes pounced, "Why should anyone do that? You said she had no enemies."

Hewitt had evidently not previously made this connection and he said slowly, "Enemies of my father's then. But I am convinced that Mother never ran away with anyone. She and Father had their differences, but she was an angel on earth and it is just not possible that she could break her marriage vows. Nor is it possible that she could be living and not have contacted me in some way by now."

Hewitt folded his arms and both Holmes and I sensed that the subject of his mother's disappearance was, for the time being at any rate, closed.

Sherlock Holmes then examined Andrew Hewitt minutely about his tumble from Grenadier, without bringing out any new facts, until he asked, "Can you recall the moments after you regained consciousness?"

"Oh, yes," said Hewitt, "I could hear Ned and my father. They were bending over me. How strange," he mused, "that they should have sounded so far away when they were so close."

"They called your name?" prompted Holmes.

"Yes, they did," Hewitt responded. "Of course they would, wouldn't they? Specially had I actually managed to make any sound when I fell. Wait a moment! I remember now, Father said -" Here he stopped short, his mouth open to speak, but instead of words he only emitted a small gasp. "No, it's gone. I don't recall anything they said," he murmured at last. "I don't remember anything."

Even I knew he was lying and Holmes could barely contain his impatience over the abrupt withdrawal of Hewitt's co-operation. With a visible effort of self-control, he placed his hand firmly on Hewitt's arm. "The truth," he said in a soft voice, "the entire truth is always better than a portion of it. If you won't speak for your own sake, speak for the sake of the lady who cares for you so deeply."

Andrew Hewitt flushed and looked away from us and then reluctantly brought his gaze back to ours. We could see the inner struggle taking place within him as respect for his parent balanced against Holmes' appeal.

At length he forced out, "Here it is then. Father kept saying, 'Damn you, Andrew!' I don't know how often, but several times anyway. And then I heard Ned say, 'Papa, don't!' And then everything went blank until Jane was there and I was in the cart."

"Your brother's words," urged Holmes. "Were they spoken with the emphasis you put upon them just now? As if your brother was telling your father not to do something, rather than consoling him, for instance."

"Yes," agreed our client, "it was a plea, a warning, something like that. But, Mr Holmes, I didn't even remember all this until speaking to you just now. Perhaps I've got such things on my brain, now that we've hired detectives and started accusing anyone of heaven knows what. But it may not mean anything. My father is a soldier and soldiers are not permitted to show affection or grief or anything that does not become a man. 'Damn you' must serve for all situations with a man like that. You do see what I'm saying, don't you? He may have been saying, in effect, 'Damn you for falling off your horse and giving me such a fright.'"

"How has your father behaved towards you since your fall?"

"I've not seen him. I don't think he likes to come here, knowing he will probably find Jane or her uncle."

"After your brother said, 'Papa, don't,' did you feel any kind of movement or a blow to your head?" Holmes stared intently, his grey eyes never blinking.

Hewitt groaned at the prospect opened by the question and muttered, "I felt nothing; I just went blank."

By this time Hewitt's face was flushed a vivid red and his breath was coming in irregular gasps. If our purpose here was to keep him from harm, I felt I had to bring the interview to a close fairly soon. "Holmes," I said, "as a doctor, I must advise –"

My friend flashed a most unpleasant-looking smile towards me. "Whenever Watson begins a statement with a reference to his medical qualifications, I know that I am in for a wigging."

"We cannot allow ourselves to forget," I pointed out, "that Mr Hewitt is convalescing from an injury. I think he needs rest before we continue with any more questions."

"Very well," agreed Holmes with a bad grace. "We'll leave off for now, Mr Hewitt. I imagine that your fiancée's company would be more to your liking than ours. Watson will stay on guard, while I fetch Miss Melrose back."

"Thank you, cousin," sighed Andrew Hewitt earnestly, when the door had closed behind the detective. "Doesn't your friend like me – or is that his usual manner?"

"It is his way. Don't let it distress you."

"It isn't so much what he says; it is those eyes of his. He suspects me of lying, but how could I, when it's clear he can see straight into my mind regardless of what I say."

I poured my patient a small brandy and, as he savoured it, the colour returned to his cheeks and his spirits seemed to rise.

"Do you know, Dr Watson," said he, "if there is a plot against me, it is clear that the stirrup was only the first part. Now Uncle Melrose has sent for Sherlock Holmes to finish the job by badgering me to death. That's right, isn't it?" He concluded with a laugh behind which I detected a note of hysteria.

I felt compelled to remind him that such a suggestion went no way to answering who had damaged his saddle.

"I know," he sighed. "It's very strange. But, as Mr Holmes says, I have to find out what happened because it matters so very much to Jane. Six months ago, I wouldn't have cared, but now everything is different. There's something to be said for being unhappy, cousin. It is the only time when one doesn't have to be afraid of losing the happiness one has. Ah - here they come. Smiling faces, all. No worries here."

THE DINNER

Holmes and I repaired to my room, which had already been aired and made ready for the arrival of Miss Melrose's 'cousin'. Since there had been no advance notice of a second guest, my friend was temporarily without accommodation, while a pair of housemaids scurried back and forth to a room across the hall, bringing fresh linen, removing dust-covers, lighting the fire and shaking rugs out of the windows. Whatever the household attitude towards the Melrose retinue may have been, all practical aspects of hospitality were being generously observed.

I took particular pleasure in the tea-tray that had been laid for us. It carried sufficient sandwiches and dainties to satisfy any three men, but I was determined to give a good account of myself. Holmes, as so often, appeared to take no interest in the food, other than to gaze at me as I munched on one of the hearty sandwiches. However, I had taken a skimpy and hurried breakfast on his account and was not to be intimidated by his looks, when I had travelled so many miles on such a raw day.

While I continued to eat, he circled the room in his nervous way. I reckoned it as snug and comfortable enough, but Holmes paced around it like a prisoner seeking a way out, fingering the tester and the draperies, patting the overstuffed chairs and opening all the various drawers and doors in the chest and wardrobe. His search through the writing table ended in an exclamation, and he waved a sheet of paper at me.

"It is the same paper," he declared, "upon which the note to Miss Melrose was written."

"Then anyone in the house may have written it," I rejoined.

"Any well-educated, right-handed man in the house, Watson. I should be tempted to add that the writer was no older than fifty, were it not for Miss Melrose's description of Colonel Hewitt as a vigorous man."

I pondered my friend's dictum for a second before answering, "Assuming the other Hewitts are right-handed, then the note was written by one of the three. But that was the probability all along. What have we learnt?"

"It is never unimportant to confirm the obvious. Every fact that is known for certain is like a channel marker in these treacherous waters." Holmes tucked the paper into his inside pocket and took a seat in a chair opposite mine. "I fear that hard facts will be a precious commodity in this household. We dare not trust the father or the elder brothers because they are the most likely suspects. Miss Melrose and her uncle can tell us little as they have only met the family this week and have been excluded from the family circle for most of their stay here. And then we have Andrew Hewitt, who thinks his mother must be dead because she has not written to him."

"Do you not believe that she is dead?" I asked.

"Surely it is obvious what happened. The father was decoyed away by a spurious message. The mother and her lover went off in the opposite direction to make good her escape, first giving a bottle of wine to the driver, who she knew quite well could not resist his tipple."

"But what about the driver's death?"

"The direct result of his inability to guide a horse over dark lanes once he had consumed the liquor. An unfortunate accident. Doubtless the purpose of the drink was to delay him or to render him useless to anyone who might question him as to the whereabouts of his mistress. In the event he was rendered speechless forever, rather than simply for a few hours."

I felt bound to stand up for the lady, murmuring that her son had claimed her to be a virtuous women, but Holmes brushed my objection aside.

"He is a loyal son. He cannot face the truth. He tells these lies to himself and repeats them to us. Consider, Watson, why else should a woman's disappearance be allowed to go unquestioned? She was of a prominent local family, and had the county police seen the slightest evidence of foul play they would have been quick to follow it up. Had the Colonel or any one of his sons believed that she was dead, would they have been satisfied until the matter was properly investigated?

"Well," I protested, "if she had been killed, whoever killed her would have been perfectly satisfied to let the matter drop. If Colonel Hewitt had wished there to be no investigation, would it not have been an easy matter to write a note that supposedly proved a rendezvous and explained his wife's disappearance?"

Holmes grinned and shook his finger at me. "Oh, Watson, Watson, you are developing a suspicious turn of mind. I fear it is my doing. Nevertheless, your point is valid. We have not yet learned enough to draw any intelligent conclusions. And we must not allow the very interesting case of the mother to distract us from our real purpose here. Now, as for Hewitt himself -"

His thoughts were interrupted by a rap upon the door, followed by the diffident head and shoulders of Heywood Melrose, the insurance man. "I am sorry to disturb you, gentlemen," he began, "But I wished to learn if you had any early insights into our conundrum, Mr Holmes."

I invited him in and offered him a cup of tea from my tray. Holmes proffered the chair upon which he had been sitting and retreated to the bed, where he propped himself against the headboard with his long legs stretched out in front of him. This had the effect of distancing him from the conversation even while he took part in it, for, though he could easily speak to us, Melrose had to lean round the back of his chair to see Holmes at all. The businessman therefore addressed himself primarily to me.

Holmes settled himself comfortably and led the conversation off by saying, "We cannot tell you much, of course. We could not find the stirrup leather any more than you could. As to who might have removed it or why - it is too soon to speculate. And yet this household is a chilly place, do you not agree?"

"Very chilly. If I had my way, I would take my niece on the next train back to London and let this family of hearty sportsmen go to the devil. If I may speak frankly I don't see why butchering natives in India and collecting rents from tenant farmers in Somerset should be a nobler calling than providing incomes for widows and orphans in London. And I don't intend to take much more of their high-handedness. As if a niece of mine had to scheme for a part of their fortune; it makes no sense. If it was money she was after, wouldn't she set her cap at the eldest boy, rather than the youngest? If anyone should be accused of fortune hunting it is Andrew Hewitt. He knows I never had any children of my own and that Jane stands to inherit my nest-egg when I pass on. He does himself no harm by a match with her - no harm at all."

I felt this was being unfair to Hewitt and said so.

"His sole virtue," snapped Melrose, "is his apparent devotion to her. But what is a man like him good for? He's as nervous as an over-bred lap-dog and not very much more intelligent. He will not stand up to his father even to defend the woman he says he loves. Those two hours I had to spend alone with him this afternoon passed like a fortnight. Talk - the lad can talk, and no mistake about it. If only there was a grain of sense in a single thing he said. When I think of the splendid fellows Jane has turned down and then see her bowled over by a boy with nothing but a pretty face; it's maddening, that's what it is!"

Melrose was not an attractive sight when he was agitated. What little family resemblance he bore to his pretty niece was lost in the folds of his heavy dewlaps and the curl of his upper lip. Throughout this diatribe he had wagged an emphatic index finger so close to my face that I had drawn back involuntarily several times to save my sight. A glimpse of Sherlock Holmes' serene features reminded me that he had dealt with Heywood Melrose in the past and had, I suspected, chosen his position on the far side of the room with the man's conversational quirks well in mind.

As Melrose paused for breath, Holmes commented in one of his more obvious understatements, "You sound as if you might welcome a severing of the engagement every bit as much as the Hewitt family."

"Not quite so much as that, Mr Holmes," Melrose smiling mirthlessly was even more unattractive than Melrose in anger. "I am not willing to do anybody any harm. But, yes, if I thought I could persuade Jane from this marriage, I would talk until doomsday against it. I have held my tongue as I know her mind is made up. She loves him: there it is. My disapproval would only drive her away from me and then who would she turn to when she discovers her mistake?"

There was an uneasy pause, which I ended by asking, "Mr Melrose, who do you think is responsible for Andrew Hewitt's fall?"

Melrose sipped his tea before answering. "I don't know

for sure, of course, but if I had to guess at a culprit, my money would be on the father. It's clear he despises his youngest son. Wait till you see the two of them in the same room and you will understand what I mean. Besides, no one moves in this house except by the Colonel's command. Maybe one of the other sons actually cut the leather and one of 'em might have picked it up to conceal the crime, but it was all at Colonel Hewitt's will, mark my words. I wouldn't be upset at seeing the whole bunch of them brought to book for it, either. Well, I probably said too much. I shall leave you gentlemen in peace to work out the solution to this mystery."

With that, he set down his teacup and left. As the door closed after him, Holmes gave a short bark of laughter, before plumping up the pillows, making himself comfortable and going to sleep on my bed.

§§§

Holmes and I did not meet the rest of the Hewitt family until we were seated at the dinner table that evening. As additions to the Melrose party we were spoken to with a civility that had nothing in it of warmth or genuine hospitality. Colonel Hewitt reigned at the head of the table, with his sons arrayed on his left and right, including Andrew, who had descended from his sick-room. All the Hewitts were tall and well-made, but the father and the two elder brothers lacked the beauty of feature that was so remarkable in the youngest son. The colonel himself was the epitome of the stern military man; he had a square jaw and eyes sharp and as cruel as any bird of prey. His receding hair and bristling moustache were iron-grey, while his voice had the timbre of one whose commands were to be obeyed without question.

It needed no great effort of imagination to suppose that Andrew Hewitt owed his good looks to his mother's side of the family and, as I glanced around the room, I immediately saw confirmation of my theory. The portrait of a woman, who could only have been the Colonel's wife, hung upon the wall opposite his place at the table. An Irish ancestry was more apparent in her face than in her son's, but there, unmistakably, was his sharp chin and those exotic and luminous green eyes. It seemed sad that her portrait should oversee the family feast when she herself was no longer present. Thinking it might be a delicate matter with the family, I had intended to make no comment upon the painting, but Andrew Hewitt saw the direction of my gaze.

"That is my mother," he said proudly.

"What a lovely woman she was," I said. This seemed safe ground, since it was undeniably true. "Did you paint the portrait?"

"I rarely do portraits, as I really have no talent for it. But she wanted so much for me to do it, and it did turn out rather nicely, I think. My subject inspired me."

Colonel Hewitt interposed. "My son disdains portrait-painting as a rule because it smacks of respectability. Were he to be admitted to decent houses to paint portraits, he might risk the loss of his bohemian brethren. He might even turn a profit by his efforts. Life would lose all romance for him."

Andrew flushed slightly, but kept silent in the manner of one who has long since resigned himself to the futility of arguing. His tactic was successful, in that his father said no more on the subject, moving on to other matters, such as the venality of the government, the hounds run by one of his neighbours, and the likelihood of good weather for the next meet.

The meal was suitable for a trencherman and it struck me that even Sherlock Holmes must add something to his girth should our investigations at the Hewitt household occupy any great length of time. But the hearty fare could not disguise the guarded air of hostility that emanated from the head of the table to surround us all. The dining room itself was not conducive to warmth and good feeling: although this was the lesser dining area, meant for intimate family gatherings, we were not a sufficient number to fill all the places at table. An attempt had been made to spread the eight of us evenly around the board, but the distance thus placed between individuals only accentuated the lack of family feeling in our assemblage.

Above all, the room and the company suffered from a dearth of feminine presence. Miss Jane Melrose, lovely though she was, seemed a lamp turned low, casting more shadow than light. Intimidated by her future husband's family, she spoke in subdued address only to her fiancé, her uncle and to me. How I wished that the lovely woman from the portrait above us could have given her the companionship that would have set the room singing with womanly laughter and conversation.

I was in the midst of this daydream when Colonel Hewitt turned himself abruptly towards Sherlock Holmes. "Am I to take it, sir, that you have appeared in my home as a witness for the character of my son's future bride?" he demanded.

"Not as a witness, Colonel Hewitt," replied Holmes smoothly. "That would imply that she is on trial. No, sir, since I am a friend of both Miss Melrose and her cousin, Dr Watson, here, I made so bold as to add myself to your son's kind invitation to his ancestral home. I hope to see some more of his work while I am here, also."

"His playground is in London. You would have done better to stay there," our ungracious host growled.

"I am referring to his early work. Besides, I would be honoured to take part in your next hunt."

The Colonel seemed mollified by this last remark and said, more genially, "I am told you are something of a horseman, Mr Holmes, so they say who saw you by the paddock this afternoon."

"I have done a bit of riding in my youth, though I find less and less opportunity for it now. This looks to be splendid galloping territory."

The Colonel mellowed even more and there followed a lengthy discourse on the local hunt and its followers, their horses and the hounds, to which Holmes added such questions and comments as to keep the old soldier going in that direction, although he needed little urging to talk of what was clearly an obsession. I recognised in Holmes' line of inquiry a quest for some basic information about the locality and its residents, but in any case I was vastly relieved to have the burden of conversation carried by my more fluent friend. I had worried that I might fare badly were I pressed to act my character as Miss Melrose's cousin in any depth.

And then, just as I was breathing easily, the colonel asked Holmes if he had ever served Her Majesty in the military service. Holmes disclaimed such a past, but lightly remarked that I fitted that particular bill.

"Indeed, sir," said Hewitt, turning a friendly countenance to me for the first time. "I am curious to know when and with what regiment."

As briefly as I could I explained the circumstances of my army service. At first our host reacted with the standard fighting man's disdain at a mere army surgeon, but his manner changed after he had pressed me to identify the units to which I had been attached. "Am I mistaken, sir, or were you and the regiment not present at Maiwand for that terrible encounter with Ayub Khan?"

"I was there," I explained, "but cannot claim to have distinguished myself. I was wounded early on and played but little part in the events of the day."

"Don't bow your head, man. Chance is the ruler of every field of battle: some are wounded, some are slain and some rise to heroism. The point of honour is, did you stand your ground and do your duty by your country and the men who stood beside you?"

"For so long as I was able, that I did," I responded with pride in my voice.

"There you are. I raise my glass to you. My sons will do the same. You see now, Andrew, how a man may find a way to serve without himself wielding a weapon. You might have become a surgeon, like Miss Melrose's cousin here. Surely your refined and artistic hands would not lack the skill for the surgeon's knife. All that's wanting is a little courage and the willingness to sacrifice for your fellow-men."

I was embarrassed beyond words and could only send young Andrew Hewitt a look of the most sincere apology for having been the indirect cause of yet another rebuke from his father. The unfortunate man again showed no trace of the resentment that might have been expected and let the taunt pass in silence. Nevertheless, the whole table felt his humiliation for him and there was an awkward stillness for some minutes.

Across the table, Sherlock Holmes looked pensive; then a sparkle of light danced in his eye, and I knew there were squalls ahead. "A little courage and the willingness to sacrifice were qualities wanted by the cavalry at Maiwand, I think," he offered blandly.

"I could not agree with you more," said the old

warrior. "It was a disgrace for them to stand apart when brave men were fighting against such odds. Had I been there, I should have tried what steel and horse might have done to the enemy's flanks."

"And yet, perhaps, even such a charge would have made little difference."

"Little difference! Why, I have seen fifty determined horsemen carry the day against thousands."

"A slight exaggeration, surely," twinkled Holmes.

"It is no such thing. And may I ask," asked Colonel Hewitt, bristling, "what experience you have of such matters that you may give your opinion so freely?"

"I am a student of history," said Holmes. "I do not deny that your first-hand knowledge is superior, but I maintain there is something to be said for detached study."

"A battlefield is no place for study," responded the soldier brusquely.

"Maybe not in the heat of action, but afterwards - it would do our officers no harm to consider the consequences of what they have done or failed to do in that action. For example, I suggest it would be instructive to see exactly what you might have done differently at Maiwand. I wonder if you have a map of the area close to hand? No." He said briskly as the soldier shook his head, partially in bewilderment. "Suppose I were to draw a rough outline for you."

To my amazement Holmes tore a page from his notebook and began to sketch the territory I remembered only too well. Colonel Hewitt leaned down the table to see better; he seemed more than a little irritated with his guest, but he was as willing to join an argument as Holmes was to provoke one, and it was not long before the two of them were huddled over the makeshift map, bickering over questions of terrain, the ideal spot at which to charge, the proper moment to use pistols versus sabres, and various other points of mounted tactics. The rest of the company were silent, dumbfounded that any guest should have the temerity to subvert dinner conversation into a pitched battle, while I experienced the additional shock of discovering that my friend possessed a wealth of knowledge upon a subject which I had never known to be of the slightest interest to him.

As the debate progressed, Colonel Hewitt's voice grew louder and his face redder, while Holmes retained that bland composure of his which I knew from my own experience was more maddening than any display of emotion could be. It struck me that Holmes was becoming increasingly and deliberately argumentative, disagreeing with his host simply for the sake of giving a contrary view. Suddenly Hewitt had had enough; he slammed his fist on to the table with a force that set the silver dancing. Edward Hewitt sprang from his seat and was between the two in an instant, counselling peace.

Holmes gazed around at us in apparent surprise. "I seem to have offended you, Colonel Hewitt," said he with outrageous understatement. "I never intended so to do. I am sure that your knowledge is far greater than mine on this subject. Pray accept my apologies and let us by all means discuss something else."

The older man resumed his seat with a grunt of exasperation. "Very well, Holmes," he said. "Your apology is accepted." But for the remainer of the meal, whenever he glanced at Sherlock Holmes, it was with the look a man might cast towards a horse which had bitten him – full of resentment, wary, and determined to have the better at the next exchange.

I was left with only one further impression from the family gathering that evening, and it was puzzling. Throughout the meal, the eldest son, David, remained almost completely silent, responding only when courtesy demanded a word or two from his lips. For the most part he kept his attention upon his father, but there were odd moments when I caught his gaze fixed upon Miss Mclrose. Unfortunately, his features were not expressive and I could not read the meaning behind his look. Was it of admiration or disdain? I saw that Holmes observed it also and wondered what he might make of it.

After the meal we men repaired to the billiard room for cigars and brandy. To my further embarrassment Holmes began to boast of my skill at billiards, giving such embellishment to my small talents that the Hewitts were soon on fire to test me. Holmes himself declined to participate and, indeed, seemed quite overcome by boredom after only a few minutes, so that I was neither surprised nor unduly disappointed when he made his exit with Andrew Hewitt in tow, explaining that he wished to see more of the painter's handiwork.

With the departure of the two men who were irritants to the master of the house, the evening became more pleasant, concluding with Colonel Hewitt extending an invitation for me to ride with him and his sons on the morrow for some light exercise, the following day being the next hunt meet. I accepted without hesitation, pleased that I seemed to have come into favour with the old and distinguished soldier. It was only when I returned to my room that I realised that it might have been a dangerous mistake to agree to such an excursion without Holmes' approval, but, as the hour was now late and I saw no light under his door, I decided not to disturb him.

THE NOTE

In the morning I looked in on my friend and found him still abed, though fully awake. He had propped himself up with several pillows and was sorting through a pile of photographs and papers.

"These are the articles Andrew Hewitt showed to Miss Melrose immediately after their arrival here," he explained. "Hewitt and I went over them together last night, but I thought it would do no harm to look through them once more without his presence."

"You think that they may point to something that led to the attack on Hewitt?" I queried.

"I cannot afford to ignore the possibility," said Holmes, still turning over pages. "But I see I am keeping you from your ride," he made a gesture towards my boots and breeches. "Who goes with you?"

"The Colonel and the two elder sons."

Holmes clapped his hands in delight. "Excellent, Watson! I had feared that the watchful Mister Edward would never leave the grounds while we are here. Now listen carefully: should Edward or anyone else wish to leave the group, you must find a way to get back to the house first to warn me. What a pity," said he with a whimsical smile, "that you haven't a hunting horn to sound, as they did in the old ballads."

Another idea sprang to his mind and he darted to one of the drawers in the massive oaken dresser by his window. "You may not find the opportunity to play this card, Watson, but then again, you may. We cannot afford to waste any chance or we may find ourselves spending an inordinate number of draughty nights in this high studded fortress. Take this with you. It is the mysterious and highly offensive note received by Miss Melrose. Would you please try to spend a quiet moment with Mister David Hewitt, during which you may freely communicate your displeasure over his offer to your cousin."

"Are you certain that David is the writer?"

"Not absolutely certain, but the probability is decidedly with one of the two brothers and the elder is the more likely to have sufficient resources to carry out his promise. In any case, David was so quiet at dinner that I feel we scarcely know him at all, beyond his apparent fascination with your pretty cousin."

I was open-mouthed. "Do you think he may be attracted to her?"

Holmes grinned sardonically. "That would be one explanation that would encompass both the note and an attempt to do away with brother Andrew, would it not? However, if admiration of Miss Melrose were in itself a sufficient motive for crime, I should have serious suspicions in your direction, my friend."

I was affronted – and said so.

Holmes ignored my protestations and simply handed me the paper. "Now take the note, won't you? Your confronting David Hewitt with it is sure to draw him out to some extent, whether or not he is the author. I want you to be persistent, Watson. Abandon your customary amiable nature and express yourself strongly on the subject of your cousin's honour. Press him until you get what seems to be a heartfelt reaction from him."

"Should we take the initiative in this way?" I asked, not at all happy with my proposed part.

"We must take it whenever we can, Watson, which is why I bedevilled the Colonel at his own table last night. It taught us that the well-respected old gentleman has a somewhat volatile temperament and that his son, Edward, is well aware of it. Now, you will see what you can learn about the eldest son. At the worst, if we can draw a little attention in our way, it will be that much safer for our friend, the painter."

"Shall I take my revolver with me?" I asked.

Holmes laughed. "I doubt that you will find yourself in any immediate peril – but you will remember to check your saddle and bridle before you mount, won't you?"

With which warning as my only comfort, I descended to take my place among the three principal suspicious characters of our investigation and ride with them alone out of sight of all witnesses or help. Which of these three gallant horsemen had written the ungallant note which sought to buy an end to Andrew Hewitt's engagement to Jane Melrose? Which of these strong fellows had weakened the stirrup leather of the youngest son's saddle?

Which of them had concealed his own or his relation's evil deed by taking up the leather from where it had fallen? And what could have possibly motivated the attack? Was it greed, family pride or perhaps some long-nourished family hurt to which none but the injured party now attached any importance?

And yet, as we rode along through woodland and across meadows, the thought of evil just dispersed into the raw March wind that swept along the rolling landscape. The overcast sky of the previous day was with us still, but on the western horizon there appeared a hopeful streak or two of sunnier days. Colonel Hewitt expressed his opinion that good weather was due for the meet, and no one chose to dispute it.

It may have been an odd thing for him to do, since he had such objections to the union between 'my' family and his, but the old colonel seemed determined to give me an informed tour of as much of his land as could be comfortably ridden in a few hours. On one lovely hillside, where we passed the overgrown ruins of some ancient stone cottages, he bade us all rein in our mounts while he discoursed on the practice of enclosure of the nearby lands for pasture, which had caused the abandonment of many a hamlet in earlier centuries. He showed me the cider apple orchards where he hoped to raise a crop that would protect his prosperity against the plummeting price of corn. He told me stories of previous generations of yeoman Hewitts and, at very slight urging from me, gave a full account of the action at Rashesh, for which his name was so worthily renowned.

In fact, Laurence Hewitt had served in both Sikh wars and had stories to tell of Mudki, Ferozeshah, Ramnagar and the rest. To hear him tell it, he had been loath to leave the military when he had fallen heir to his estate and, after a few months leave to organise his late brother's affairs in 1853, had rejoined his unit in India and remained to serve in various skirmishes during the Mutiny. In the end, however, the responsibility of the ancestral home, affecting as it did not merely his own family, but a goodly portion of the West Country as well, caused him to resign his commission at last and return to the peaceful life of the country land-owner. Small wonder that the hunting season meant so much to him; it must have been his only excitement in this humdrum rural life that fate had forced upon him.

It happened that both the Colonel and I had tried our hands - or risked our necks - at the sport of pig-sticking and we exchanged a number of anecdotes on this subject as our leisurely ride permitted. All in all, I found it hard to keep Holmes' warning in mind, save that the silent reserve of the the two sons reminded me of my less-than-welcome status among the Hewitt clan. It occurred to me at last, when I was in the midst of telling one of my stories of camp life, that the old soldier was possibly drawing me out to affirm or disprove the claims that I had made the night before.

Certainly no one made any move to do me any harm, neither on windy pasture or in misty glen, and I returned to the stableyard at Coombehill uninjured, except for the muscles in my body that had in recent years adapted themselves more to chair and sofa than to the back of a moving horse.

It was not until we had left the horses with the groom that I saw my opportunity to speak alone to David Hewitt. The Colonel had remained behind for a conversation with old Pratt, and Edward Hewitt had rushed off on another of his errands, leaving me to walk back to the house in the company of the eldest son. I had already determined how I would open the discussion and it was as well I had my lines prepared, for Hewitt's initial look of disdain would have stifled any casual conversation.

"I have an idea this belongs to you," I began, handing him the folded note. "My cousin, Miss Melrose, found it in her room and she does not wish to retain any communication which so obviously could not have been meant for her."

He glanced at the piece of paper and shrugged as he put it in his pocket. "I see it took her three days to decide it was not for her."

Even without Holmes' instruction this answer would have been more than sufficient to bring me to an argumentative state. The arrogance expressed in the downward curve of his lips was in itself a red rag.

"She saw immediately that it was none of her business,

but the delay lies in the decision as to whether she should ignore the insult or confide in one of her relations and seek the apology that is her due."

"I don't see any need to apologise," sneered Hewitt. "It was a handsome offer, had she cared to enquire any further."

"Handsome!" The effrontery of the man took me by surprise and it was with the greatest difficulty that I restrained myself from giving the young puppy a thrashing. Even as I felt my knuckles clenching, I knew that Holmes would prefer a lengthy conversation to fisticuffs. Pushing my anger down, I carefully said, "I would be curious to hear how you justify such an offer to a lady."

"It really is very simple, Dr Watson," the fellow threw a particular emphasis on my honorific title and gave a light laugh. "My youngest brother has done his best all his life to disgrace the family name, but this intention to marry a person from the stage surpasses all his previous escapades. I could hardly let the matter pass without making what effort I could to prevent it."

With a struggle, I kept my voice polite. "My cousin is a lady of complete respectability and great accomplishment, who would be a worthy wife for any man."

"Oh, I'm sure that in her circle she is well enough respected - among banking clerks and military surgeons who like to grace themselves with the title of Doctor."

I am renowned for my equable temperament, but my reputation was in question at this moment. I suspect David Hewitt realised that he had gone too far, for he stopped in his tracks and, as I swung back to confront him, he waved an airy hand. "Well, then, let 'em marry. Let them. They are marrying for love. Pshaw. The pretty pair of 'em! Was there ever such folly as that inspired by a pretty face. I'll tell you what, my dear doctor - why don't you ask my brother to tell you about my fiancèe? I think the story should be of interest to your fair cousin. Then ask our merry-andrew where his mother lies tonight. Now good day to you - doctor."

§§§

I let him go and returned to my room. There Holmes was waiting, his eyes alight with excitement. "Close the door," said he as I entered the room. "I have something to show you. But, my dear fellow, how cross you look! Sit down here and tell me your troubles, while I help you out of your boots."

I told Holmes of my conversation with David Hewitt. As I spoke, I began to see the funny side of it and, encouraged by Holmes at his most genial, was even laughing by the time I reached the end of my narrative.

"This is most interesting," observed Holmes when I had finished. "Master Andrew never gave us any indication that there was such a lot of bad feeling between himself and his brother. But then the story of David's fiancée does not sound as if it will be much to Andrew's credit."

"David is still a bachelor, of course," I pointed out. "It takes little imagination to see how a brother with Andrew Hewitt's looks might distract a young woman from her original choice."

"And the taunt about the mother. Mark that well," said Holmes sitting back contemplatively in his chair. "Clearly brother David takes the view that she abandoned her husband and family. But now for my news." Reaching inside his coat he withdrew something coiled, which he snapped to its full length with the flourish of a circus ringmaster.

"The missing stirrup leather!" I cried. "Where did you find it?"

"In the top drawer of the dresser in Edward Hewitt's room. We are indeed fortunate that he had found no chance to dispose of it. Under normal circumstances, I should have left the evidence where it was, but I could not examine it properly there, not with a houseful of servants. As you can see, this curious break in the leather wants a careful analysis."

I took the strap in my hand and studied the broken ends. One edge of the leather had clearly been weakened by a disorderly series of small nicks, while the remainder of the break consisted of a ragged tear, which had obviously occurred at the moment when the rider had tried to absorb the shock of the jump.

"What do you suppose was used to make these cuts?" asked my friend.

I examined them again before speaking. "By their

appearance they were done with a narrow-bladed punch or chisel. But what does it matter?"

"Why not use the blade of a pocket-knife, for instance?" queried Holmes. "What gentleman goes anywhere without his pocket-knife? Why should he go out of his way to use a distinctive tool when he might have used the sort of knife that anyone might carry?"

"Perhaps," I suggested, "he carries a combination knife. Many of those carry a kind of punch or awl. But in any case, you found it in Edward Hewitt's room: he is your man."

"Not necessarily. It would not be the first time that evidence was arranged in such a way as to incriminate an innocent man. There is definitely something on Ned Hewitt's mind. However, even if it was he who removed the leather from the ground and hid it away, that does not mean it was he who weakened it. He may be protecting someone else."

For Holmes to have offered a solution, but then to have surrounded it with ifs and buts, put me in despair. "Then we are no further forward than we were before you found it."

Holmes chuckled. "It is not as bad as that, my dear fellow. By the by, how was your ride this morning?"

"Most enjoyable. Colonel Hewitt is a congenial old buffer when you get to know him a little better. And when one does not bait him deliberately."

"You have ingratiated yourself nicely," congratulated Holmes. "If nothing else, you will be regarded as a credit to Miss Melrose. What did you and the congenial old Colonel discuss?"

I enumerated the range of subjects we had touched upon during the ride.

"Had you any opportunity to speak with the sons - other than your brief encounter with the elder, that is?" pursued Holmes.

"Only in the most superficial way," I replied. "They seem to defer to their father as a matter of course - for fear of offending him, I think. There is something forbidding about him, like so many men of character and leadership. You, for example, Holmes."

"What," exclaimed my friend. "Do you mean you are

frightened of me?"

"No, of course not. And yet - I would not like to put myself on your wrong side, if you see the distinction."

"You explain yourself admirably, but do you consider the colonel -"

He was interrupted by my door being assaulted from the outside by repeated blows of a heavy fist. Holmes calmly rolled up the stirrup leather and thrust it into his pocket. Then he nodded to me to admit our visitor. When I pulled at the knob I was nearly bowled over by Edward Hewitt, whose former cool demeanour had been replaced by a state of anger that made me think how like his father he looked.

"I'm glad you're both here," he announced, heeling the door shut and striding into the room. He regarded us with black brows, looking from one to the other as if he were trying to compose himself before launching his verbal attack. "I don't require long explanations. The truth can generally be put into a very few words and I assure you I only require the truth from you. Let me first be plain with you, so that you see how matters stand." As he spoke he was calming down and his words flowed the more easily. "As I suspect you may already know, my brother Andrew has something of a history for making rash decisions, particularly as far as the company he keeps. Yesterday, when it seemed to me that your actions were not entirely what one would expect of ordinary house guests, I took it upon myself to wire to Scotland Yard in London to see if they had ever come across a Sherlock Holmes or a John Watson. My answer came this morning while we were out riding. An Inspector Gregson gives you both a good character or I should have you both run off my father's land immediately. But I think I am within my rights to demand to know why the Melrose family have engaged a private detective to investigate my family's affairs. I will not have my father hounded by enquiry agents, I can tell you that without reserve. Perhaps you might begin your explanations by telling me if my brother is aware of who and what you are?"

In front of such a confrontation, I knew well enough to defer the burden of response to my friend. This time, however, he unnerved me by giving me a look of the most intense exasperation. "I told you so, didn't I, Watson? If I had simply told the truth about my occupation from the beginning, we could have saved ourselves this embarrassment. Now I am put in the worst possible light and the very thing you feared has happened in any case. Yes, Mr Hewitt, I am a detective and well known to Scotland Yard, as you have discovered. I was all for saying so at the outset, but Watson thought that it might make the family uncomfortable if they knew my line of work. However, I am not here on business at all. I came with my friend Watson here - surely Inspector Gregson told you that we are old friends - to serve as an ally to him and to his dear cousin. I confess that the prospect of riding to hounds was an irresistible inducement and I had my own share of curiosity concerning Miss Melrose's choice of husband. Andrew is certainly aware of my usual occupation. As to my deception, you may have gathered that I was never in favour of it. While it is true that many people find themselves uncomfortable in the presence of a detective, it only makes matters worse when they consider themselves deceived as well. We should all be open and honest, Watson, and should have spared Mr Hewitt all his trouble. Now I fear he will never trust us. You are a careful man, indeed, sir. I have never known a host who would telegraph to Scotland Yard to prove the identities of a couple of houseguests."

Edward Hewitt seemed somewhat taken aback, as I had been myself, by this speech, but he began to bluster. "I told you that my brother is easy prey for bad influences. He has no judgement in such matters."

"If you are referring to my cousin Jane..." I reacted angrily, but Holmes laid a restraining hand on my arm.

"Now, Watson, let us try to see Mr Hewitt's point of view. He simply needs to know that he has nothing to fear from us. Are you satisfied now, Mr Hewitt? If you like, I am willing to confess my occupation to the entire household at luncheon today."

Edward Hewitt peered at Sherlock Holmes as if to search his countenance for some clue to his true intent. It was plain that he believed not one word Holmes had said, but it was just as apparent that he could do nothing about it. "No," he answered at last, "you are most likely correct to conceal it. My father is fond of his privacy, as you may gather from the fact that we spend all of our time here in the isolated countryside. Since you are out of favour with him already, Holmes, it might be as well to leave matters as they are. Good day to you both." He turned on his heel and left the room abruptly.

As the door closed behind him, Holmes patted my shoulder approvingly. "Oh, that was nicely put, Watson. 'If you are referring to my cousin Jane'," he repeated in much the same tone of voice that I had used. "Master Edward may doubt my word - in fact, I'm sure he does - but he was convinced by your anger, and it stops him short of doubting that you are Miss Melrose's cousin. I fear I have misjudged your talents as an actor!"

"Thank you, Holmes." The detective pays me few enough compliments, but I was bound to qualify the encomium. "But I was truly angry. How could I help it? The Hewitt family's attitude towards Miss Melrose is simply outrageous."

My friend's face fell. "You think so, do you? You miss the point, Watson. We are not here to settle family quarrels, much less to take either side of them. We are here to solve one crime and to prevent another - if there is to be another. What is Miss Jane Melrose to you, after all? Until yesterday you knew her only as a name on a playbill. I believe you are taking your role as her cousin much too seriously. It won't do, my friend. She is a client and she is nothing more and, if you cannot keep that in mind, I suggest that you return to London and leave the matter to me."

Holmes glared at me until he was satisfied that I was sufficiently chastened and contrite. "I shall do my best to remember what you have said," I murmured.

"Good. Still, even your faults happen to have helped our cause. And your regard for Colonel Hewitt - now, don't deny your high opinion of him - may grant you some impartiality after all. But now, let us consider where we stand. Edward Hewitt did not mention his loss of the stirrup leather. Does this mean that he is clever enough to say nothing or that he has not missed it yet? Or, if the leather was placed in his dresser by another hand, he may not ever have known it was there."

"Why should he contact Scotland Yard if he were himself guilty of a crime?" I asked.

"Bluff, perhaps. Or fear."

"Fear?"

"Oh, yes, fear. It is the fearful man who constantly looks over his shoulder for pursuers," opined Sherlock Holmes.

THE GARDEN

The food at luncheon was again excellent and we might have been a jolly party indeed had the conversation too been so rich and varied. As it was, Colonel Hewitt held forth, David seemed sulky, Edward looked distracted, Holmes said not a word, and the rest of us laboured along as best we could. After we had taken coffee, I was eager to join Holmes outside for a stroll in the fresh air.

"What a family gathering we are, eh, Watson?" he laughed. "I have seen more merriment dancing to a funeral bell, haven't you? I do hope the loving couple plan to set up housekeeping in London and not anywhere near the groom's family."

"I understand that Andrew is in the process of buying a house near Russell Square," I said.

"Farewell to the bohemian life of the artist, is it?"

"I doubt that the artist had to live in a garret if he was taking five hundred a year without selling a single painting," I pointed out.

"True," Holmes accepted. "Let us bear towards the summer house. I have asked Melrose to meet us there. Before I searched the bedrooms today, I let him into the office where the Colonel keeps his business records. There he is. What news have you for us, Mr Melrose?"

Melrose started guiltily before welcoming us into the summer house and placing upon its table a notebook. As he opened it he said, "It was just as you thought, Mr Holmes. The Colonel and his eldest son do the accounts themselves, and all the essentials were in the desk."

"I trust you left everything as as you found it," Holmes admonished. "I had no chance to rejoin you after my own investigations were concluded."

"I was very careful," said Melrose stiffly, smoothing down a page in his notebook that was covered with notes and calculations. "I could never have imagined the wealth of the Hewitt estate. They seem to own half the county and, although they had to reduce the rents last year because of the weakness of the market, this has enabled them to retain nearly all of their tenants and keep their income steady. Such shortfall as there was has been more than made up by their interests in the port of Bristol. The cost of the estate is heavy, with all the servants and a stable full of horses, but the annual income more than covers the expense, while the capital investments assure the Hewitts should keep unassailable hold on their wealth until at least the next generation."

"You found no signs of questionable dealings?" quizzed Holmes.

"None. Colonel Hewitt is just a good man of business. I had supposed that he was merely a soldier who had come into his wealth by sheer accident, but it's clear that his management has enriched the family wealth beyond what his father or his father's father ever dreamt of."

"What of the other items I asked you to look for?"

Melrose turned a page and said, "You were right on the mark there, Mr Holmes. There was one item: a quarterly payment of £15 to a Mrs Sally Collins."

"A tenant of the Hewitts?"

"She lives on his land, in a place called Spring Green Cottage, but she doesn't appear to pay any rent. Well, I suppose it would be pointless for her to pay in when he pays out so much to her."

"For how long has this arrangement existed?" asked the detective.

"The first payment was made in the January of 1880," said Melrose, after referring to his notes.

"Some three years. Did you make any other discoveries of any moment?"

Melrose turned another page. "You ought to know that Hewitt gives a tidy sum to the village church and to various other local charities. It also appears that he keeps the local medico supplied with the latest in medical equipment and anything else he might need."

"Dr Farthingale, you mean," I interposed.

"Yes, indeed. Colonel Hewitt made him a present of a brand new gig only last year."

"I don't suppose you were able to find any private correspondence during your search?" Holmes enquired hopefully.

Melrose shook his head. "It was all business that I saw."

"You have done well," Holmes congratulated him. "You seem to have a natural flair for detective work."

"I should hope that I could follow any reasonably well-kept books," sniffed the insurance man. "I would be a poor man now had I never learned to do so."

Holmes chuckled. "Nevertheless, your knowledge has been of great value. Do you happen to know where your niece planned to spend her afternoon?"

"I saw her not ten minutes ago, arm in arm with the young Gainsborough heading towards the croquet lawn."

We took our leave of Melrose and took the shortest route along the garden walk between rows of established rhododendrons. In another month or so they would have made a charming corridor of lavender blooms, but now their dark green leaves looked bare and bleak. We were about to emerge on to the open lawn when Holmes' arm suddenly shot out in front of me, bringing me to a halt.

"Look there," he whispered, pointing through a gap in the tangle of branches and dead leaves. Two men who had emerged from a side door of the house were engaged in a heated conversation. One was Edward Hewitt, the other, judging from his advanced years and his medical bag, was Farthingale, the country doctor. I say the conversation was heated, but, in truth, all the anger appeared to emanate from Hewitt, while the doctor's every gesture expressed surprise and denial.

"I cannot make out a single word," growled Holmes. "If we step out they are sure to see us. There is no cover at all."

"The discussion is over," I observed.

Edward Hewitt's face was clearly visible as he crossed within twenty yards of us, but we need not have seen his clouded expression to read the fury in every stride. For his part, the doctor proceeded on his way around the corner of the house, his destination probably the same as our own. Holmes signalled that we should quicken our pace and, by so doing, we overtook Dr Farthingale just as he came upon Andrew Hewitt and Jane Melrose, who were sitting together on a bench in a leeward niche in the mossy wall. Hewitt, though bundled up in a cap, muffler and overcoat, was sketching bare-handed upon a pad, while the lady watched. As we approached she had just pointed out something of amusement in his work and, with their faces lit by laughter and their devotion to each other, I doubt there could have been a more handsome couple in all England.

They caught sight of the three of us and, in short order, introductions were performed all round. There was a fatherly warmth in the doctor's manner towards his patient, an affection openly returned by the younger man.

"I am delighted to see you looking so well, my boy," said Dr Farthingale. "This beautiful young lady has taken excellent care of you."

"Yes," returned the artist. "She has even been so diligent as to make sure that she has a cousin who is a doctor, so as to keep a medical man constantly on my case. What are you hiding under your coat, you old fox?"

"It is a gift to the Hewitt family." So saying, the doctor revealed a black and white kitten which had been nestling in the warmth of his ulster. "I cannot take any credit for her, however. I have merely provided her transportation from the stables of Underhill to the stables of Coombehill, where your neighbour, Sir Gerald, hopes that she will earn a reputation nearly as fearful among the local vermin as the late lamented Ajax."

"How very kind of Sir Gerald." Hewitt put out his hand to receive the cat, who promptly sank her tiny needles into his fingers. "She has the proper high spirits of a mouser," he laughed. "Pratt will be pleased to see her. Our current staff of felines are woefully indifferent performers and he swears the stables will soon be overrun if we do not get some sterner stuff as soon as possible. Do you want to hold her, Jane? Mind her claws."

Even Sherlock Holmes unbent enough to chuck the tiny creature under the chin and he smilingly said, "I trust that this harmless kitten was not the source of Edward Hewitt's ill-humour towards you, Dr Farthingale."

The doctor looked sharply at Holmes, while Andrew Hewitt glanced anxiously at each of us in turn. "What ill humour?" asked the artist. "What has Ned been saying to you, Dr Hugh?"

The doctor dissembled. "I don't know that I should repeat it to anyone but you, my boy. It was a most extraordinary accusation. Completely inexplicable. Most extraordinary."

"Speak freely," urged Hewitt. "We are all friends here.

And do sit down: I have forgotten all my manners. There is room here beside me."

"Your brother sought me out and followed me through the side door. He demanded to know why I had set detectives upon his father. When I said that I had no idea what he meant, he called me a liar. I am simply baffled by it all."

"How ever did my brother find out you are a detective, Mr Holmes?" demanded Andrew Hewitt of my friend.

"The news is spreading rapidly," responded Holmes with a bitter smile.

"Oh, lord, I have irritated you again, haven't I, Mr Holmes? Is it because I have as good as told Dr Farthingale that you are a detective? I have no secrets from my trusty old friend, have I, Doctor Hugh?"

"I hope you never do," responded the doctor with a twinkling eye.

"Mr Holmes, this man has been a friend to me when I most needed one. It can only help to confide in him." Receiving the most grudging of nods from Holmes, Andrew Hewitt briefly explained to his friend our purpose in coming to Coombehill.

Dr Farthingale shook his head sadly. "A bad business. Even if we could imagine anyone capable of such a deed, why should it be now?"

"Mr Holmes thinks that someone may wish to keep me from marrying Jane," explained Hewitt.

"Excuse me, doctor," interjected Holmes. "What did you mean by the phrase 'Why should it be now?'. Was there ever a time when Andrew here might have been expected to be threatened with danger?"

"Well," said the old man with some reluctance, "there was some bad feeling after his mother's disappearance."

I noted that Andrew Hewitt went quite white and that his clutched hand made Jane Melrose suddenly wince.

Dr Farthingale must have also noticed the young man's reaction, for he clapped his hands together and announced, "Now, why don't you two take a turn through the gardens and I shall tell Mr Holmes the whole story."

After very mild protestations the couple left us and Holmes and I took their place upon the bench next to the country doctor. As we sat down, I studied him closely.

He was a man of about sixty, upon whom years of hard work and irregular hours had left their mark in rough, weathered skin and hands that were deformed by arthritis. There was a hoarseness in his voice that he tried to clear from time to time, but his cough was dry and useless.

"Before you begin, doctor," said Sherlock Holmes, "may I ask how long you have known Andrew Hewitt?"

The lined face drew itself into a tender smile. "I brought him into this world. He knew me years before he saw his own father. Oh, he was a jolly, strapping lad with a ruddy face and a head full of black hair. Gave his mother some difficulty at his birth, he did, being so big and she being something of a small-boned woman. But she managed, with a bit of assistance from me. What a dear boy he was. Handsome, merry as a cricket, clever with his hands – he was the joy of his dear mother's life. Ah, those were happy days when Bess Hewitt first moved to Coombehill. I shouldn't say so much, perhaps, considering it was only possible because of the death of the Colonel's brother. And yet it was the work of a wise Providence to remove this estate from that ne'er-do-well and put it into the hands of Laurence Hewitt. The Colonel is a fine man, and I say so to this day, despite the grudge he bears me."

"Is this related to his problems with his youngest son?" asked Holmes, a touch of impatience in his voice.

"Yes, oh, yes. The trouble began well before Bess Hewitt disappeared, you see. Young Andrew was always closer to his mother than his father. He had inherited many of her gifts: a love of beauty and a gentle soul foremost among them. Another sort of father might have cherished such a son, but not the hero of the Sikh wars. By the time the Colonel resigned from the army and came home to meet his son for the first time, the boy was already five years old and accustomed to his mother's gentleness. The other boys seemed to take the change in the household in their stride, but then, they are more like their father. The break came for good when the Colonel insisted that the boy pack up and go to university. Only his baggage went where the Colonel sent it. The boy himself went to Paris instead and stayed there eighteen months to study his painting, as he had wished to do all along. It was Andrew's own notion to do it, but naturally his mother was not going to to see him go hungry once he was there, so she sent him money at regular intervals. The Colonel could do nothing about it, for Bess Hewitt had her own nest-egg. Her money gave her boy his independence, but it put an irreparable rift in the marriage, as you may imagine, especially when Andrew returned home. From then on, there was always an argument at Coombehill between man and wife, father and son, brother and brother. Wait a minute - I've left out something. The business over that foolish girl."

"Which foolish girl was that?" asked Holmes, quite as if we had no idea.

"Now, what was her name? Oh, no matter! To tell the truth, I don't know the whole story, but she had been engaged to David, and then she turned up in the summer house one evening in Andrew's arms, so the tale goes. I think there was too much made of it. Any young girl with eyes in her head would be drawn to Andrew, not to mention that there is more life in him than in his two brothers together. Still, she let David propose to her, and that ought to mean something, shouldn't it? David has never forgiven his brother, though he ought to have been grateful to him. Why, the girl was more changeable than the weather, and she threw away the chance to be mistress of Coombehill one day, just for the sake of a few kisses on a summer evening with a lad far too young to return her affection."

"How long ago was this incident?" asked Holmes.

"At least a dozen years. Yes, that's right, because Andrew was seventeen, I remember that. Well, I only tell you about it because it shows the kind of thing that has been going on within the family. Then three years ago, when Mrs Hewitt disappeared, the rest of them seemed to give up all efforts at getting on together. Andrew was devastated by it all, of course. A terrible thing to happen to a sensitive lad. In the weeks following the disappearance, he alternated between states of bitter fury and hopeless despair. During the bitter moods he made some regrettable, possibly unforgivable, accusations towards his father."

Holmes murmured for him to elaborate.

"He made reference to his mother's unhappiness and to his father's jealousy. He implied that his father - the boy was ill, you understand, and most of what he said had no logic to it. He was desperate for an explanation for the loss of the person he held dearest in the world and it was easier to accept the worst idea that logic could invent than grasp the truth that we shall probably never know what became of her."

"Was Colonel Hewitt truly a jealous man?" asked Holmes.

"He is a possessive man by nature and his wife was very, very beautiful, even after thirty-seven years of marriage. She married quite young, you know, and was only fifty-five when she vanished."

"Did you ever know the Colonel to be violent towards his wife?"

"Oh, no. As her doctor, I think I would have seen the signs."

"What think you of the idea that the Colonel may have done away with his wife?"

The doctor shook his head. "Most unlikely. Andrew would tell you the same, now that he is quite himself."

"What was the Colonel's response to his son's accusation?" I asked.

"He turned the boy out of the house. Not even Ned's attempts at reconciliation could sway him. The Colonel told his youngest son he never wished to see him again."

"What, then, did he do?" I persisted.

"He came to me," the doctor said simply. "He was far from well and, though he might have gone around the world on his income, I could not leave him to fend for himself. He would scarcely touch food for days on end. He had no interest in life itself for some time."

"It was good of you to show such concern," I said softly.

"I was happy to do it," said the doctor, "for his lovely mother's sake and for his own. And it was a change from living alone, even if he was not his customary light-hearted self. I've been a widower these past five years, you see. However, the price I paid for looking after Andrew was to lose the trust of the rest of the family."

"They seem to have reconciled their differences with

Andrew, if not with you," commented Holmes.

"There never was a reconciliation. There were no apologies made, no explanations given. Time just passed and the subject of the rift was seldom mentioned. Andrew had gone to live in London once he was well enough to manage on his own. One day, about a year and a half ago, Edward suggested that Andrew should come home for a short visit. The Colonel accepted his presence without comment. Andrew arrived, stayed in his old rooms, rode his horse, played billiards with his brothers - all as if nothing had ever happened."

"And the Hewitt family has continued to sustain your practice," Holmes voice carried a small question.

"Yes, I should never be able to stay if they did not. Be assured they do not do it for my sake, but for the good of the countryside at large. Colonel Hewitt takes very seriously the responsibility of a great landowner. But how could you guess at this?"

"Miss Melrose's uncle told me," said Holmes without qualification. "Now, Dr Farthingale, since you are so close to the family and must have your own ideas, what do you think has become of Mrs Hewitt?"

"It is useless to speculate. No one knows anything," replied the doctor with a shrug of his shoulders.

"It is certain that someone somewhere does know," said Holmes, "but tell me, did she ever speak to you of a wish to leave her husband or this place? Even in the most general terms?"

"No - well - when Andrew was in Paris she once or twice mentioned a wish to go there. But that was to see her son, not to leave her home. I cannot think that she ever intended to leave. I believe her to be dead. I believe it because Andrew believes it and he was closest to her. He has told me that in his heart he knows she is dead and I know that such deep feelings are generally accurate. Further, as a practical matter, what would have induced her to go away without telling her beloved boy? He would have done anything for her; he would have lied for her, helped her on her way - anything. And she knew it."

"Is it not possible," asked Holmes, "that he has lied for her, as you suggest, and done it well enough to convince everybody?"

"That is precisely what Colonel Hewitt does believe and that is the source of the quarrel between them. The Colonel is certain that Andrew has been in contact with her. But the boy's confusion and grief over her disappearance were genuine, without question. No, he believes her to be dead."

"Very well, then, if she is dead, how do you suppose it happened?" Holmes enquired.

"The only thing I can imagine is that she was set upon by some stranger or strangers to the district. Collins managed to break away in the cart, leaving his mistress to her fate. In his own terror to escape, he drove the cart right off the road and, since he is dead, we shall never know if that is true."

"Were there any strangers seen around here about that time?"

"Not that I ever heard of," the doctor acknowledged, "but that's my whole point. They got away unseen. If they had killed someone, they might well have made sure they did, that's for certain."

Holmes looked as if he was going to argue with this rather nebulous hypothesis, but then clearly decided this was going to be a waste of time and changed the subject slightly. "Did you examine Collins after his death?"

"Yes. You see, Andrew thought he was still alive when he found him with the wreck of the cart and so he came to fetch me. However, the man was dead when I got there: a broken neck. There were no other marks to speak of - a few abrasions from the trees and bushes that he struck when he fell, nothing more."

"Had he been drinking?"

"Without doubt," averred Dr Farthingale.

"And you absolutely reject the notion that Colonel Hewitt might have killed his wife?"

"Absolutely. It would be entirely out of character. In any case, although you might not know it, the Colonel had witnesses to his movements for most of that night."

Holmes looked interested and invited further comment by his attitude.

"The local Superintendent was quite thorough in asking his questions. I think he must have spoken to every man, woman and child in the villages for ten miles around. But what bearing can all this have on Andrew now being in danger? Can anyone truly mean to harm him?"

Holmes looked grave. "It is a possibility."

"If there is anything I can do to help, just let me know. There they are coming out of the garden. Shall I wave to them that we have finished our talk?"

"Please do."

The doctor signalled to the young couple. As they strolled towards us, he continued. "I find it hard to imagine the Hewitts could be responsible. What do you think the motive is - to prevent the marriage?"

"If that is the motive," said Sherlock Holmes, "then their efforts come too late. Andrew Hewitt and Jane Melrose are married already. And Edward Hewitt, for one, knows that they are. Is that not so, Mr and Mrs Hewitt?"

THE STIRRUP

"How in Heaven's name did you know that, Mr Holmes?" marvelled Andrew Hewitt.

Dr Farthingale and I were as thunderstruck as he, but Miss Melrose – Mrs Hewitt, I should call her – blushed and smiled knowingly.

"I can only suppose that Mr Holmes must have followed you last night, my dear. Am I right, Mr Holmes?"

Holmes bowed his head to the lady. "Precisely right. Of course, I must hasten to tell you that my intent never was to discover your secret. I feared an attack on your husband and made it my business to stand guard when you and your uncle left him alone for the night. I followed him until I saw his destination, but after that I knew that I need not keep watch on him any longer."

Hewitt laughed nervously. "We were married in London a fortnight ago. And you are correct again – Ned does know about it, because he was there."

"We have confided in no one else," added his wife. "Not even my uncle. Perhaps you don't realise that he was not very much happier about our engagement than Andrew's family. I know we should have told you, but, with all that has occurred, we thought it better to keep the secret among as few people as possible."

"You could not be more wrong," said Holmes. "I want you to tell everyone the truth at dinner tonight."

"I would rather tell my uncle in private," said the lady.

"Very well, Mrs Hewitt. My main concern is that we remove the marriage as a possible motive for harming your husband. Especially if he intends to ride tomorrow, I should prefer to keep a limit on the number of persons who might have reason to harm him."

Dr Farthingale shook his head angrily at young Hewitt when he heard Holmes' mention of the hunt. "Don't tell me that you intend to ride tomorrow, Andrew?"

"It will be my last chance before the autumn and I can't miss it. Poor Grenadier will think I have forsaken him entirely. I feel perfectly fit today and I am sure I shall be even better in the morning."

Both Farthingale and I did our best to explain to our

mutual patient the dangers of forcing the pace of recovery from a blow to the head, but Hewitt stood firm. At one point I looked to Holmes for reinforcement of our entreaties, but he had taken up the new kitten and seemed completely absorbed in playing with her. I could only surmise that it suited his purpose somehow if our client was to risk his neck on the morrow. Once it was clear that all argument was useless, the elderly doctor took his leave, embracing Andrew Hewitt and his bride with many wishes of health and happiness.

As the doctor turned at the end of the path and waved, Andrew Hewitt said to Holmes, "Did you find out what you wanted to know from the doctor?"

Holmes shook his head. "Your mother's disappearance clearly divided the family and its acquaintances, but I cannot understand why it should take three years for this division to lead to an attempt on your life, if that is indeed the case."

"I told you it made no sense, Mr Holmes. My mother has nothing to do with it."

"I could wish that you had been more honest with me from the first. Both of you. When your wife told me that the family were 'at odds' that was a rather deceptive understatement of the events described by your friend the doctor. I take it that your wife knew the truth of it."

"Oh, yes, weeks and weeks ago," Hewitt said, smiling fondly at his new wife. "It was only fair to show her all the dints and chinks in her knight's shining armour."

"That is all very well," Sherlock Holmes sounded mildly exasperated, "but now, Mr Hewitt, tell me once and for all, have I heard the entire truth of this family, of your mother's disappearance and of your own recent fall?"

Hewitt nodded emphatically. "Of course. I confided everything to Dr Hugh; he knows all my secrets."

"Very well," nodded Holmes. "Let us see if we may not confront yet another member of your family with the truth. Mrs Hewitt, I hope you will excuse us, but I think Edward Hewitt will be more inclined to speak freely in your absence."

"I'll go and give the kitten to Pratt," said the lady cheerfully and, giving a brief kiss to her husband, departed towards the stables.

Holmes inclined his head towards her departing back and abruptly asked Andrew Hewitt where his brother might be found at this time of day. On being told the library, we all bent our steps thereto. We found Edward Hewitt in the library as his brother had predicted. He was at the far end of the room, sitting in an armchair before a small fire, smoking his pipe in the attitude of a man who seeks to regain his composure after a period of some stress or anger. He twisted about in his chair as we entered and the smile of greeting that came to his face at the sight of his younger brother was quickly replaced by the stern and guarded look that he had worn in all his prior dealing with us.

"What can I do for you gentlemen?" he asked in formal tones.

"Mr Holmes wants to speak to you, Ned," said his brother.

Holmes gestured to me to close the door behind us. As I did so, the elder brother gave us a crooked sort of smile. "This must be a serious matter," said he. "Will you sit down? Let us all sit by the window."

We arranged ourselves in a small semi-circle of chairs in the bay window, looking out on to a formal Italianate garden. I thought that Holmes would begin whatever he had to say immediately, but he kept silent, staring intently at Edward Hewitt until all of us felt completely ill at ease.

"Well, Mr Holmes," said the barrister at last. "Have you seen enough of me? Have you anything to say?"

"You may speak first, Mr Hewitt," replied Holmes quietly. "I should like to hear what you have to say on the subject of this piece of leather."

Edward Hewitt was nothing if not self-possessed. He took the incriminating strap from Holmes' hand with no more show of surprise than had he been given a mildly interesting volume from the bookshelves around us.

"So," quoth he, "you've been through my room, have you? These are polite houseguests you've brought us, Andrew."

Andrew Hewitt had been taken aback at the sight of the missing stirrup leather and the implication that his brother had concealed it struck him a second blow. While he floundered to give voice to a single intelligible thought from the many that seemed to clamour to be spoken, Holmes pursued the conversation as if he was entirely unaware of his confusion.

"You admit that you removed it from the ground where your brother fell?" asked Holmes.

"I can hardly deny it, since you have undoubtedly found it among my things. Why," said Edward Hewitt with a touch of hauteur, "did you search my rooms?"

"Because I believed I would find the stirrup leather there," said Holmes. "Now tell me - and your brother - why you removed it and concealed it as you did."

"I took it so that my father would not see it. Look here where the rats had been at it. I knew Papa would be in a fury that one of the stable lads had not taken proper care of the saddle, so I put it in my pocket hoping he wouldn't find out. But obviously my simple action has been misconstrued and someone, presumably your Jane's uncle, has called in an investigator. What nonsense!"

Andrew Hewitt seized on this. "If my saddle was damaged by rats, then it means that no one is trying to kill me."

"Kill you!" exclaimed Edward Hewitt. "Land's sakes! Of course not! I only hope you haven't got that old busybody Farthingale on the scent as well."

"You yourself accomplished that," Holmes said.

"Well, damn the old meddler, what else could I do?" Edward Hewitt expostulated. "Andrew, you'll tell him it was all a misunderstanding, won't you? We don't want him poking his nose in again, do we?"

"He was only trying to help me, Ned," said Andrew. "I don't know why you all hold it against him so."

"Oh, my dear brother," Edward Hewitt waved a dismissive hand, "let us spare these two gentlemen our five hundredth repetition of this disagreement over old Farthingale. Are you satisfied about the stirrup now? And will you tell your new relations to send their detective back to London?"

Sherlock Holmes seemed amused. "Your brother will be the happiest of men when he can be rid of me, I should think."

"I have nothing against you, Mr Holmes," said Andrew

earnestly, "if you will only stop asking all those painful questions about things far outside the scope of your investigations. You are satisfied that Ned has told you the truth, I hope?"

"Yes," agreed Holmes, "I think that completely settles the matter of your recent fall."

"That's splendid then," Andrew cried, leaping to his feet. "You'll stay for tomorrow's meet, won't you? Even my father wants to see you ride to hounds. Cousin Watson, of course must stay. And tonight I shall tell everyone about my marriage. There will be no more secrets here." As he spoke he darted from one to the other of us, clapping our shoulders and shaking each of us by the hand.

"Very well," smiled Edward Hewitt, with affectionate amusement at his brother's sudden high spirits. "Except in the one instance, Andrew: you must not tell Papa about the rats. And it would probably be as well that no one else should know that Mr Holmes is a private detective, don't you agree."

"Not a word on either subject," promised Andrew. "I'm off to tell Jane that our troubles are over. Didn't I say as much, Mr Holmes? Once we spoke to Ned, everything would be cleared up. And it is - it has been!"

Away he dashed to his wife, but we lingered behind, Holmes still holding the stirrup leather, the cause of our presence at Coombehill. Edward Hewitt glanced at it and shook his head.

"I am truly sorry that you had to come all the way from London for nothing, gentlemen. It is a strong reproof to us that our new in-laws think us capable of harming our own relation."

"It was worth a journey simply to set the suspicions to rest so quickly," replied Holmes. "I am surprised that you should go to so much trouble to protect one of the stable lads, Mr Hewitt. If he was not caring for the saddles in the proper way, he deserves to lose his place."

"It might not be that easy to determine which boy is at fault," countered Hewitt smoothly, "and we cannot afford a general sacking while the season is in progress."

"And then there is your father's quick temper, eh?" said Holmes. "Miss Melrose - Mrs Hewitt, that is - thought her father-in-law was extremely upset over the accident and the injury to Andrew."

"He was. He is capable of speaking most unkindly to Andrew, but he loves him deeply. He was as distressed as I have ever seen him when my brother fell that day. The poor old lad just lay in a heap on the ground, not moving at all. I most certainly did not want my father to see that damaged leather while my brother's condition was in doubt. I never dreamed that the Melrose family would send for a detective to investigate an ordinary riding accident."

"There were a few peculiar circumstances," Holmes said mildly. "For example, why did your father curse your brother as he lay half conscious?"

"Papa curses whenever he is upset. It was always his way. You will never see him shed a tear over a sorrow; he will show anger instead."

Holmes nodded. "My friend Watson is much the same. And your cry of 'Papa, don't!'. What made you call to him in that way?"

For once Edward Hewitt seemed startled by a question. His reaction was not dramatic - it was no more than a slight blinking of his intelligent blue eyes - but there was no mistaking his confusion. "My brother is mistaken. He himself said that, not I."

"Ah." It was truly marvellous the meaning that Holmes' expression and tone of voice could impart to a single syllable. Had he said the words 'How very interesting, but I don't for a moment believe you,' he could not have expressed himself more plainly than he did with that brief sound. And yet, by not uttering the words themselves, he allowed the listener to draw his own conclusions based on the contents of his own conscience.

Edward Hewitt blushed slightly at the temples. "I am telling you the absolute truth, Mr Holmes. You imply that my father did something for which a reproach was warranted, but he did not. I was there, and I believe my brother would allow that I was in better possession of my senses than he was at the time. Let me tell you what truly happened. My father was holding Andrew in his arms; cursing him and calling to him by turns. Suddenly my brother opened his eyes and cried out as you have said, 'Papa, don't!'. He immediately lost consciousness again."

Holmes nodded as he listened to this account, seemingly satisfied now that he had heard the truth. "Andrew's memory must have played a trick on him. But you see now why he was susceptible to the idea that someone meant him harm?"

"Of course," Edward Hewitt seemed mollified. "There's always the meddlesome old doctor to feed him suspicious nonsense."

"What made you think that it was Dr Farthingale who had retained my services?"

"He is capable of anything. I know what you are thinking: he seems such a kindly old man. In fact, he was a great family friend until my mother's disappearance, and then he seemed to turn against us. It was as if he blamed us for it somehow. I'm sure it was he who filled my brother's head with all those fancies. I don't know if you have been acquainted with my brother long enough to observe that he is quite susceptible to fantastic suggestions of all sorts. He hasn't a particularly logical or discerning mind at the best of times, much less in an impossible situation like our mother's disappearance. He was so close to her and her loss was so mysterious, that he became prey to that mean-spirited old man. And so factions were formed: my father and my elder brother form the desertion faction, while Andrew and Farthingale are what might be called the murder faction."

"And you, Mr Hewitt? Which faction do you favour?"

"I lean towards the desertion faction," Hewitt said seriously, "with one qualification. My father and brother believe that Andrew helped my mother run away or, at least, that he knows where she is. This I know to be untrue. My younger brother may at times have difficulty giving the proper balance to fact and fancy, but he is no liar and he is absolutely incapable of shamming the kind of anguish that he endured after she left us. He truly believes she is dead, poor chap."

"His argument is," said Holmes, "that her character was against her just leaving."

"I'm sure we all thought so, but she often went to London, ostensibly to see her mother and sister. It is possible she met someone there without arousing any suspicion here at home. My mother was a gentle soul, but she had her own very definite views on many things and she often defied my father quite openly. Who can ever say what a woman is truly thinking?"

"But you knew of no particular admirer," said Holmes.

"Certainly I knew of one," averred Hewitt, "but she didn't run off with him, that's plain. Everyone knew that old Farthingale was in love with her. But, Mr Holmes, I hope that you don't intend to investigate my mother's case now that you have nothing else to occupy your attention?"

"I find the circumstances intriguing," admitted Holmes. "I regret I was not consulted three years earlier."

"I doubt that it would have made any difference. She is gone for good, I fear. Once I thought it would help if we knew the truth of it, but now – well, we have got over the worst of it. Suppose you were to discover where she is? How would my father feel? How would any of us feel? It will not make matters any better to harp on the subject and torment ourselves. You cannot imagine what agony Andrew went through during the first weeks after she had gone. He is only now getting over the shock – some of the credit must go to your cousin, Dr Watson. I suppose she **is** your cousin, Dr Watson?"

I hastened to answer, "Oh, yes." I suppose I should have told the truth then and there, but I could not bear to bring even that much discredit upon Jane Hewitt. I saw Holmes raise an eyebrow, but he did nothing to correct me.

Edward Hewitt appeared to accept my word. "You understand that I had my doubts because I could not recall seeing you at the wedding."

"No, I was not there," I dissembled. "I had business away from London and could not cancel on such short notice."

"The speed of it took us rather unawares," added Holmes mendaciously.

"But," I said, "there is no doubt they are very much in love. I am happy to learn that you of all the family were not opposed to the match."

"How could I oppose it once I saw them together?" Edward Hewitt apparently spoke with feeling. "When I saw my dear brother light-hearted once more, after so much sorrow. I trust you will not take offence if I tell you that I would not care a jot were your cousin a scullery maid, if she can go on making my brother as happy as he is now." His voice broke over his last words and he had to struggle to finish the sentence. "I am very fond of my brother. Don't make him go back to that awful time three years ago, Mr Holmes. Leave well alone."

Holmes bowed his head. I suppose that Edward Hewitt believed that he was expressing agreement and assent.

§§§

I offered no objection when my friend suggested another turn around the grounds. The raw days in March may suffer in comparison to the softer weather of April, but, after a cold and wet winter, I was glad enough to welcome even the hint of spring, if not its actual arrival. Since Holmes seldom walked aimlessly, except when he was distracted by a problem, I concluded that it was not mere chance which brought us back to the bench where we had found Andrew and Jane Hewitt earlier. The artist was alone now, sketching industriously at his pad, but he looked pleased to see us again. I was finding it part of Hewitt's charm that he nearly always looked delighted at the prospect of company and conversation, in contrast to the reserve one often encounters in the English.

"Is everything settled with Ned, then?" he asked, pushing his cap to the back of his head and beaming merrily at us. "He really is a splendid fellow, you know, though he is my own brother!"

"He thinks the world of you as well," I said.

His smile beamed even brighter. "Well, I told you to trust him, didn't I? Everything he did was with the best of intentions for me and for Father. Why, Ned doesn't even like to see the servants unhappy if he can help it. You are not angry that there is no crime to solve, are you, Mr Holmes? Don't worry about your fee; Uncle Melrose is too honourable a fellow to hold back your money after getting you all this way from town to help us. And I'm so pleased with the outcome that I would like to match his payment myself. I'm sure we owe cousin Watson something for his medical advice, as well."

"We have a system of dividing Holmes' fees between us," I hastily explained. "If you are so generous as to double the amount, that would more than cover my charges."

"I would prefer to earn my money," Holmes interrupted coldly. "You have another mystery here which has never been solved. Watson and I are at your service if you will but say the word."

Hewitt's whole posture drooped visibly at the mention of this topic. He brooded over his sketchpad for a few moments and finally, without looking up, he mumbled, "That is a mystery which can never be solved."

Such a statement was a challenge to Holmes, who dropped to the seat beside Hewitt and put an eager hand on his arm. "Let me see what I can do," he implored. "If it can be done, I am the man to do it."

Hewitt covered the detective's hand with his own, though he never raised his eyes from his drawing. "That's kind of you to offer," he said. Then, taking a deep breath, he dared to look at the determined face beside him. So powerful was the force of Holmes' will that I saw in the artist's eyes a momentary impulse to accept the offer. In the next instant, some wave of sorrow and fear had washed away his resolve. "If I thought she were alive," he groaned, "I would beg you to find her. But as it is I cannot do anything."

"I hope the man you are protecting is worthy of your loyalty;" Holmes observed.

Hewitt looked deeply shocked. How many times had I seen Holmes surprise the truth from an unwary subject with just this approach, but Hewitt, though he was forever disparaging his own intelligence, was not such a fool as to give anything away. "I think he is," was his quiet answer. "And if you know that much, then you see where I stand."

"Should you change your mind," said Holmes, "you will let me know?"

"I promise you," said Hewitt, "but I'd rather talk about something else. The hunt, for one thing. I've been thinking - or, to be honest, I've been listening to my wife - and she doesn't think it would be a good idea for me to do any hard riding tomorrow. After listening to a brace of doctors who agree with her, I have to admit that it might be wiser to follow the hunt a little more slowly. It would be rather pleasant for a change, bringing up the rear in a cart with Jane beside me. It would be a good way for her to meet all the locals, you know. What I'm getting round to is that I'd very much like you to ride Grenadier tomorrow, Mr Holmes."

"I would be honoured," said the detective. "I was about to ask your permission to ride him this afternoon, as a matter of fact."

"You won't run him hard, will you? Save that for the hunt."

"I won't run him at all. Watson tells me that I missed some glorious views by not going with your father this morning and he wants to show me around a bit."

Hewitt gave me a grinning sidelong glance. "Don't run Dr Watson too hard either, Mr Holmes," he said in a stage whisper. "I thought he was showing signs of being a bit saddle-weary. Ask Pratt to saddle old Gertie for you, cousin. She's very smooth-gaited. Shall I see you both at tea?"

"I doubt it," said Holmes over his shoulder as we hurried away.

THE COTTAGE

It was only a matter of minutes before we were riding down one of those Somerset lanes that would, come high summer, be ablaze with montbretia. My heart could not have been lighter than at that moment: Holmes had solved the mystery, Andrew Hewitt was safe, and there was not even the slightest need for a feeling of remorse for the villain. Stable rats! Stable rats and a well-meaning brother had combined to give the appearance of a crime. Now the case was closed and there was no reason not to enjoy the countryside and to breathe in the country air. How pleasant it is to ride on horseback beside a close friend, knowing that conversation is unnecessary, but companionship is ever at the ready, should one desire it.

I had let Holmes choose our path and his unfamiliarity with the neighbourhood caused him to lead us down one of the less promising lanes. We soon found ourselves on a narrow and muddy track, where the bramble grew as high as our horses' ears and sent out treacherous green stalks that threatened to pluck the caps from our heads. As tactfully as I could, I suggested to my friend that we might do better on one of the lanes that I had travelled with the Hewitts that morning, where we could ride unencumbered and view some of the countryside as well. There was no response from Holmes.

Looking over, my heart sank. Though his cap was pulled down nearly obscuring his eyes from my look, there was no mistaking the set of his jaw and the determination in the poise of his head. He had not heard me because he was deep in concentration, and he could only be immersed in such serious thought when he was working out one of his problems. This ride of ours was business, not pleasure.

I tried a more direct approach to rouse him. "Holmes," I ventured, "where are we going?"

This he acknowledged. "I have a fancy to see the Widow Collins' Spring Green Cottage."

"The Widow Collins? Of course!" I exclaimed. "Collins, the groom! The mother's disappearance! But Holmes, we have been urged not to investigate the matter."

"True," he agreed. "I suppose that is the very reason

which makes me inclined to pursue the enquiry. Did you know that I rode to the village this morning?"

"I wonder that you had the time," I commented, "with everything else you appear to have done."

"I rode rather quickly," admitted Holmes. "I called on the local constable, a likable fellow named Johnson. I confided to him my name and profession and, though he was reserved at first due to my status as an amateur, we soon found that we had much to talk about concerning crime, criminals and the benefits of punch on a raw day. Somehow we got to talking about Mrs Hewitt's disappearance; one thing led to another, and I found myself treated to a look at the files. It seems Johnson never much cared for the way the case was handled, but he could not go around his Superintendent, a dolt named Bellows, who spends most of his waking hours fawning over the prominent local families."

"Including the Hewitts?" I prompted.

"Especially the Hewitts. Johnson wouldn't go so far as to say that his superior is dishonest or genuinely incompetent, and yet - if you are agreeable, Watson, I should very much like to submit the facts for your consideration as well."

"Please do." It was almost as if we were sitting either side of the fireplace at Baker Street, rather than ambling along a Somerset lane.

"Good," Holmes said crisply, his facts readily marshalled. "On the twenty-first of October in 1879, Mrs Elizabeth Hewitt left her home at Coombehill and journeyed to a neighbour's house some four miles distant. She was driven in a small two-wheeled cart, pulled by a single horse. It was Mrs Hewitt's custom to do most of her visiting in such a humble conveyance, because she did not wish to flaunt her wealth and position, and because she was apt to find herself overcome with nausea when riding in a closed carriage. James Collins, a groom on the estates for more than five years before that date, was entrusted to drive her. The weather was fair.

"Mrs Hewitt's destination was a house called Primrose Hill, at that time inhabited by a couple by the name of Dudley. The wife, whose Christian name was Norah, was of frail health and has since died; her husband has moved elsewhere. The purpose of Mrs Hewitt's visit was to bring some companionship to the ailing Mrs Dudley and she spent some hours with her friend, departing from Primrose Hill at 7.15 in the same cart and with the same driver who had brought her there. The cart and its occupants were last seen heading towards the gates.

"Incidentally, Colonel Hewitt spent his evening away from home as well. He had ridden to the hamlet of Fenny Burton, some three miles northeast of Primrose Hill. It is worth a digression to ensure that you understand the geography, Watson. If one begins at the end of the long drive to Coombehill and travels northwest along the Bridgwater road, one reaches Primrose Hill after a journey of four miles and Fenny Burton after covering a further three."

I nodded my understanding.

Holmes continued, "We know the Colonel spent his time in Fenny Burton drinking a couple of pints of ale. He remained there from six in the evening to a little past eight o'clock: he says this himself and it is confirmed by nearly a score of upright village folk. The Colonel passed his time in this way, because he had in his possession a note which read, and I quote, 'My dearest Bess, All is arranged for Tuesday night at seven. I shall be waiting for you at the *Red Lion*. Tell them you are visiting Mrs Dudley, and bring a bottle for Collins. That will give us several hours start. Don't fail me.' There was no signature. The note was written in block capitals by a soft pencil upon the paper that is to be found at Coombehill.

"Having waited until well past the time named in the note, Colonel Hewitt decided that there was no further profit in his vigil at the public house and therefore got on his horse and started for home. As it was natural for him to pass Primrose Hill upon the way, he called in upon the Dudleys and learnt that his wife had in fact been there until a quarter past the hour mentioned in the note. We have no record as to his reaction on receiving this information: perhaps he was relieved.

"Back at Coombehill, brothers Andrew and Edward had taken tea together in the late afternoon and seen each other from time to time all through the early evening hours. Andrew was painting and his brother was apparently in the habit of dropping in at odd moments to talk and observe progress. They went to their supper at the usual hour of eight, and were surprised to find no others of the family in attendance. Of the three missing members they were least concerned about brother David, who made something of a habit of avoiding the others at suppertime. They wondered about their father's whereabouts, but the Colonel is hardly the man who inspires anxiety on that score. Their mother's absence was another thing; she had planned to return for supper and had said so to her youngest.

"It might be as well for you to know that all the information on the movements of Andrew and Edward Hewitt has been obtained from the latter. It seems that Andrew was incapable of answering questions due to an injury that he suffered the same night his mother disappeared."

"An injury?" I interrupted.

"A nasty blow to the head: it seems he fell from his horse. But let me continue the narrative in order as much as possible. The two brothers finished their supper quickly and decided to go to look for their mother. They were not unduly worried, but imagined there might have been a crisis at the Dudleys and, maybe, some trouble with the old cart. They were on their way at a few moments past nine. They found the overturned cart less than a mile down the road, where the road bends after the stone bridge over the stream. Perhaps you recall the place from our journey yesterday."

I apologised that I could not, but pointed out that I had been deep in conversation with Miss Melrose during that part of our journey.

"Mrs Hewitt," Holmes said tetchily. "She was Mrs Hewitt even then. We will ride to the bridge again later; I had little time yesterday, since I wanted to return before all of you, but the rest of my narrative will have to wait. I believe that is Spring Green Cottage in front of us."

After the gloom of the overgrown and sunken lane that we had travelled to reach it, the cottage in the clearing was pleasantly cheery. A charming curved path of crushed stone led through a well-kept wicket gate and ended at the green door of a tidy little house of mellow stone, picked out by shutters that matched the front door. It might have been an enchanted cottage from some children's fairy-tale, it was so neat and inviting.

Even an enchanted cottage has its guard and, from around the far corner, there issued a large black dog with a stentorian bark. When he first saw us, he stopped in the centre of the yard and began wagging his tail, though he continued giving tongue in such a way as to announce our arrival to the residents of the house.

These three, a woman and two small children, soon followed from the same corner that had produced the dog. Mrs Collins, as I assumed she must be, was a tall and somewhat rawboned woman of about thirty. Her auburn hair was pulled back from her face, giving an accent to her high cheek-bones and her grey-blue eyes. By far her most attractive feature – and it would be untrue to say that she was not attractive – was the curve of her pretty mouth, which set itself into a bewitching little pout whenever she was not speaking or smiling. Both her tow-haired children, a boy of about six and a girl a few years older, had features similar to their mother's.

And each demonstrated the same intriguing reaction to us: at first, they were all smiles, but in a moment the children were clinging to her skirts and their expressions had changed to being wary. Her first words confirmed the obvious explanation. "I thought you were someone else," she said, waving vaguely at Grenadier. "You must be friends of Mister Andrew's." She was far better spoken than one would have expected from a girl in the country who had once worked as a servant.

Even Sherlock Holmes seemed charmed by her, tipping his cap quite gallantly as he introduced us and explained that we were visitors at the Hall and friends of the youngest son. "Actually, Dr Watson is better than a friend. He is cousin to Mister Andrew's wife."

"His wife!" cried the woman, clearly startled. Then she smiled, a smile as pretty as the pout. "Then the old man could not stop it."

"They married in secret two weeks ago."

There was no mistaking it. Though she was honestly surprised by the news, she was also pleased by it. Or perhaps a better way to express it would be to say that it satisfied her to hear it. It was a strange sentiment for a cottager to hold, a fact which she seemed to realise.

"I was once a servant at Coombehill," she explained. "Mister Andrew was always kind and patient to all of us there, just the same as his blessed mother was. When you see him, tell him that Sally Collins wishes him every happiness. Would you gentlemen like a cup of tea?"

"Thank you, no," replied Holmes. "If you could only help us find our way back to Coombehill, we would be much obliged. I'm afraid we have got quite lost on these twisting tracks."

Mrs Collins laughed; yes, she was an attractive woman. "You must turn right around and go back the way you came. Bear right at each of two forks and in another mile you will be in the open and can see the cupola for yourselves."

We thanked her, bade her and the children a good day, and started back down the lane towards Coombehill.

"And what was the purpose of that visit, if I may ask?" I demanded when we seemed a safe distance from the dwelling. "Was it to demonstrate that Andrew Hewitt has been to Spring Green Cottage himself?" I thought I already knew the answer to my question. How could I have failed to notice the none too subtle way that Holmes had introduced the subject of Hewitt's marriage into our conversation with the woman?

Holmes shrugged and looked away from me, as he was apt to do when it suited his plans to keep me in the dark. "It does seem to have revealed that fact," he admitted.

"She did not seem disturbed by the news of the marriage," I said, keeping to my own train of thought about his purpose in meeting Mrs Collins.

Holmes merely grunted; sometimes it could be maddening to try to talk to him.

"Well, then?" I persisted.

"Perhaps she did not see his marriage as a difficulty," he suggested blandly. "Forgive me if I have shocked you."

"It shocks me that you might take some curious pleasure in exposing such a connection. I know that you are a cynic about love and romance, but you need not try to destroy the happiness of those who do believe in such things." I felt quite indignant.

"I do not intend to spoil the happiness of any deserving

persons," Holmes retorted, "but I have lived in the world long enough to know that a pleasing appearance and an indifference to one's responsibilities can be the causes of a great deal of unhappiness for others. Ask David Hewitt if he does not agree with me completely. But I agree with you to this extent, Watson: if Mrs Collins has no actual connection with my main purpose, I see no reason to pursue the matter any further."

"What is your main purpose?" I asked.

"To find out what happened to Mrs Elizabeth Hewitt. Does that suit you better than learning who may be paying calls upon Mrs Collins?" I had the feeling that Holmes was mocking me in some way.

"Yes," I responded, "though all we have spoken to have discouraged us from delving into her disappearance."

"Of course they have," agreed Holmes. "At least one of them is hiding his guilt. You need not ask me which one of them. I do not know, but I mean to find out."

"Is it really any of our business, Holmes? We came here to see if there was any danger to Andrew Hewitt, and now we know there is not... That is, I thought we knew that. Did you believe Edward's story about the rats?"

"Oh, yes," Holmes soothed me. "That was my conclusion the instant I saw the marks on the leather. And the news that a particularly ferocious stable cat had recently passed away added to the likelihood of the rats getting to the saddle unmolested. That is exactly what still intrigues me, Watson. If the damage to the saddle was accidental - and I believe it was - then why should anyone go to the trouble of concealing it? Not to protect the good name of the stable rats, surely?"

"Perhaps someone deliberately left the saddle in a place where it was sure to attract the rats," I suggested.

"No, no, Watson. A rat is a most unreliable accomplice. It was mere chance that caused some negligent stable lad to leave the saddle in such a way that the dangling stirrup came within reach of the rodents. The probability was increased because of the death of the stable cat and because Andrew Hewitt had used the saddle recently, giving the stable lads occasion to handle it at all. But the actual occurrence was chance; Andrew Hewitt's fall was quite unremarkable in its cause."

"But in its effect –" I ventured.

"Exactly. What is remarkable about the whole case is the effect that one rather trivial incident has had on everyone's behaviour. We know that the youngest son has been at odds with the rest of the family for one reason or another since he was a very young man. When the mother disappeared the family was incapable of uniting as most families do in times of crisis. Each member has his own personal view of the events that took place and every incident seems to re-open the wounds. Watson, what did you think of Edward Hewitt's theory that Dr Farthingale had been in love with Mrs Laurence Hewitt?"

"It's not impossible," I said slowly, "given Dr Farthingale's own admission that he was her close friend."

"Why did he not tell us the whole truth?"

"Holmes," I remonstrated, "no gentleman would say such a thing to two strangers, especially now that the lady in question is – gone."

"Watson, do not mince words: she is dead. You think so and I think so. I might have believed it sooner had someone more reliable than Andrew Hewitt said so. And if she is dead, and the death has been so carefully concealed, what else may we conclude but murder?"

I pondered a moment. "Suicide? Perhaps she took herself away and ended her own life in secret."

Holmes shook his head. "It's a rare suicide who would conceal the fact. A common motive in suicides, specially those of women, is to punish the living with the knowledge that they drove the victim to her desperate action."

"Perhaps the family concealed the suicide for that very reason," I suggested.

"In that case, why not simply say she died of heart failure or a fall from a horse or an accident with medicine or a firearm, as does the rest of the world when a family member's suicide is too embarrassing to admit?" asked Holmes. "They had the family doctor in their pocket, heaven knows. He could have written whatever they wished upon the certificate, and Mrs Hewitt could rest in the family vault without any further scandal. No, Watson, suicide does not explain it."

"What about the theory that she deserted her husband and family?" I persisted.

"I cannot accept that thesis now. Not with concealed stirrup leathers and brothers up in arms over the presence of a detective. And then there are Mrs Hewitt's sketches."

"Did you find something important among them, then?" I asked.

Holmes snorted. "I finally had the wit to stop looking and simply take the drawings for what they are."

"And what are they?" I wondered.

"When a woman sings, writes poetry or novels or draws a picture, is it not true that in nine cases out of ten her subject will be a person or a place that she loves?"

"Not only women are so inspired, Holmes."

"Perhaps," Holmes granted, "but men are also apt to write histories of the world and philosophical treatises and such things inspired by their minds rather than their emotions. I have conducted a useful correspondence with a promising young scholar named Henry Higgins on this very subject."

Allowing Holmes his point I asked, "And what did Mrs Hewitt love to draw?"

"She drew her home, her sons, her husband, her garden. Why would a woman who so obviously centred her life around her home and family suddenly take it into her head to run away with someone else?" Holmes smiled. "There were no sketches of tall, dark strangers."

I clasped at a straw. "Perhaps she was leading a double life."

"Is that the impression we get of her?" said Holmes. "A former servant calls her blessed; her son and an old friend refer to her as an angel, and the worst her middle son can say of her is that she was outspoken in her views. Her husband allows her portrait to remain in the dining room, even though he believes she has deserted him for another man. Everything we have heard tells us that she was a remarkably well-loved woman."

"In that case," I asked, "who had cause to kill her?"

Holmes sat up very straight in his saddle. "That is what I feel it my duty to discover. You are, of course, free to return to London if you prefer. You would be in Baker Street in time for supper were you to ride back to Coombehill now. For my part I intend to take in the sights along the Bridgwater road."

"I should feel it worth foregoing supper if you were to continue the story of the night Mrs Hewitt vanished."

There was just the trace of a smile on his face as he acknowledged my decision. Dissimilar though we might be in so many ways, we would always be alike in the matter of curiosity.

"I had left off," he resumed, "when Andrew and Edward Hewitt had discovered the overturned cart near the bridge. The brothers say that Collins, the groom, was lying 'in a heap' about three yards from the cart. They paused only a moment beside him, intent as they were to find their mother, whom they supposed to be lying injured somewhere nearby. There had been a lantern on the cart and, though it was broken, there was enough oil in it that they were able to use it to light their search. After scrambling up and down the slope for a quarter of an hour or more, they concluded she was not there. This seemed glad news to them at the time, of course, because the clear assumption was that she had elected to remain the night with the Dudleys and had sent Collins back with the cart and a message. No written message was ever found on Collins' person or anywhere in the cart, incidentally.

"The brothers did not search for such a note at this time, however. With their mother's safety no longer an immediate concern, they turned their attention to the injured man to see what they could do for him. In the search for their mother they had stumbled across a winebottle, broken, but with some portion of the contents remaining in the thicker base, leading the Hewitts and, later, Superintendent Bellows to conclude that it belonged to Collins and that he had been drinking from it prior to the wreck. It originally occurred to them that the man might be simply drunk, but they were unable to rouse him in any way and his breathing was quick and unsteady."

I felt a doctor's experience should be brought into play. "The man was in shock, of course. A drunkard's breathing is slow and regular."

"Just so," acknowledged my friend. "The Hewitts were not so certain what was the matter with him, but they decided that Dr Farthingale ought to have a look at him. The cart had been too badly damaged to be of any use to convey the man to the doctor. Instead, Edward remained with the injured man, while his brother rode off to the doctor's residence to fetch him out to the scene."

I felt bound to comment that the Hewitts had acted with good sense and some compassion.

Holmes tilted his head in a noncommittal way. "At any rate, their part in this tale rings true thus far. It is worth mentioning at this point that Farthingale had passed part of the early evening with Mrs Dudley - from about five o'clock until nearly seven."

"He saw Mrs Hewitt there, of course," I commented.

"Oh, yes. It is not so surprising that the local doctor and the solicitous neighbour should both be in attendance at the same bedside on the same evening. In fact, Dr Farthingale had been there three times in the previous week, when Mrs Hewitt was nowhere to be found. He spoke to Mrs Hewitt for a few moments before he departed. What she told him is very odd, I think. She said that she intended to spend the night at Primrose Hill."

"But she had no such intention," I said.

"She never mentioned it to the Dudleys, that is certain. And, of course, she did not stay. She was seen leaving, you will recall."

"At seven fifteen," I recollected.

"Yes. The doctor says he last saw her at six thirty. He drove home by way of the Old Petherton Road, which is the most direct way to his house from Primrose Hill. He had not yet gone to sleep, but was in bed nodding over a book when Andrew Hewitt arrived on his doorstep. This was at ten thirty. The two men returned to the site of the accident as quickly as the doctor's carriage would travel. On the way, the doctor confirmed Andrew Hewitt's belief that his mother had remained at the Dudleys for the night and could not have been involved in the mishap.

"Neither of them was quite prepared for what they found at the scene. In the first place, Colonel Hewitt had arrived, bringing the intelligence that Mrs Hewitt was not safely at Primrose Hill after all. The Colonel seems to have been rather abusive towards Dr Farthingale, accusing him of being part of a plot to separate him from his wife. When Andrew Hewitt supported the doctor's claims of innocence, it seems to have inflamed his father still further. Edward Hewitt stopped further argument by calling attention to their responsibility to Collins, whom he feared had taken a turn for the worse. In fact, the man was dead.

"This news took some of the belligerence out of the Colonel, who dispatched Dr Farthingale to Coombehill with the body, telling the doctor that he and his two sons intended to make a further search of the area. This search was cut short, however, when Andrew fell from his horse; he had been quite overcome with anxiety when he heard that his mother was not safe with the Dudleys after all and his speech and behaviour became increasingly irrational. Neither his father nor his brother saw exactly what he did to his horse, but the animal reared up suddenly - and there Andrew Hewitt was on the ground with his head split open.

"Now it was Edward Hewitt's turn to ride to fetch the doctor. The injury was apparently quite severe and, when they had conveyed the young man home, his elder brother and doctor stayed by his bedside through the night and well into the next day. It seems to have occurred to no-one that the police should have been summoned as soon as possible. Colonel Hewitt sent a message to Inspector Bellows after breakfast that morning and, in one of the misfortunes that makes the investigation of crime such an uncertain art, the morning brought with it a soaking rain which obliterated all the tracks that might have been left upon the roads the previous night.

"There is no need to bore you with the various other points of the investigations as it was bungled by Bellows. His entire attitude was that the death of the groom Collins was a relatively minor disturbance, and he saw no reason to look too closely into whether the man's death was a crime in itself, much less its possible relation to the whereabouts of Mrs Hewitt. He accepted without question Colonel Hewitt's idea that he been decoyed away by the mysterious note in order to give his wife the opportunity to make her escape in another direction."

I murmured that that was a possibility, but Holmes shook his head.

"One of several," he snapped. "Surely it is equally

possible that Colonel Hewitt was decoyed to the pub so that Mrs Hewitt's abductor or murderer would have a clear field in the locality that night. It is also possible that the note that the police found so convincing might have been written by Colonel Hewitt himself to establish a plausible reason for his being away from home."

"But why should he do that?" I asked.

"To be seen there, of course. To be seen by a score of genuine village folk who could swear on their Bibles that he was nowhere near the place where his wife disappeared."

"Then that does, in fact, prove that he was indeed nowhere near the place and could not be responsible," I pointed out.

"Watson!" Holmes cried. "How many times have I told you that the plausible story needs to be even more closely examined than the most fantastic tale. When a man knows he is going to commit a crime, he lays careful plans. He remembers times. He can produce witnesses to his whereabouts. Think, Watson, how logical it would be for the Colonel to have an unimpeachable alibi while his agent carried out his plans to eliminate his unfortunate wife."

"What agent?" I enquired.

"Why not Collins?" suggested the detective. "Given that, you see why the death of Collins becomes even more important to the investigation. Don't forget, he was alive when Andrew Hewitt left to fetch the doctor."

"But the Colonel..." I protested.

"But the Colonel," Holmes echoed me, "might have told the groom to wait for him along the road, so that he could give him his reward for carrying out the deed so successfully. If he meant to kill him in any case, the wreck of the cart made it all the easier. Collins may have died of his injuries or he may have been assisted to his untimely death by some action of the Colonel's."

"I thought you believed in waiting for your data before formulating theories," I said.

"You are absolutely correct," admitted Holmes. "However, when there is so little data and almost no chance of obtaining more at this length of time... But no more until we reach the bridge."

The section of the Bridgwater Road on which we were

travelling runs parallel to the River Frome for a goodly distance. Then all of a sudden, seemingly on a whim, the road veers ninety degrees to the right and rises to mount the approach to a sturdy stone bridge over the river. Heaven knows what had possessed the builders to raise its height so far, when any flood level would have covered the road beyond the bridge in any case. Holmes and I rode across and turned around so that we could re-approach the fatal spot from the same direction as the doomed cart. From this perspective it was apparent that the abrupt downgrade from the height of the bridge followed immediately by the sharp left turn would make this a treacherous place in the dark of night.

We dismounted at the angle of the road and I held the horses while Holmes walked to the edge and looked down, for the shoulder of the road fell away sharply from the artificial incline created to lead to the bridge.

"If one wheel of the dogcart left the road," Holmes observed, "the vehicle must overturn, even if the cart were not travelling at a particularly high speed."

I joined Holmes and looked over the landscape. "If a person were to be thrown from such a cart it would be a miracle not to hit one of the trees below. What precisely was the cause of Collins' death?"

"A broken neck, according to the doctor. Look how the earth is soft down there because of its proximity to the stream. Had the police done their job properly before the rains began, the full story would have been here for them to read. It is another mark against the Hewitts, of course, for not alerting them at once. Nevertheless, you and I may still learn something from this place. The cart came to a stop here, I gather." He pointed to a spot some five yards down the slope. "The horse remained on his feet, but the cart had twisted on to its side with the downward facing wheel broken. The wine bottle was near Collins, who would have been approximately here. All this information comes from Edward Hewitt. Various articles had been moved by the time others began to arrive and Andrew's first-hand testimony is lacking, as you know."

I nodded, remembering that Andrew Hewitt's memory was apparently impaired after his fall.

Holmes continued, "Andrew lay unconscious all through

the following day. In the evening Superintendent Bellows did enter the sick room in the hopes of conducting an interview, but Andrew was far from lucid even then. He repeatedly asked to see his mother and seemed incapable of comprehending the questions asked of him. Two days later, Dr Farthingale took it upon himself to convey the patient to his own home, where he cared for him until he was completely recovered. Once he was well, Hewitt began to ask about his mother's fate and to question the actions of the police in the matter. Instead of seeing what Hewitt himself might be able to add to the case, Bellows merely offered him access to the files and challenged him to dispute any aspect of the investigation, if his own knowledge differed from the version that the police had heard. Hewitt read through the various depositions and said he had nothing to add, signing a sworn statement to that effect, dated 22nd December, 1879."

"Two months later!" I whistled. "Was his head injury as severe as that?"

"It seems to have been a combination of the injury and some sort of breakdown, according to Johnson."

Holmes was retreating into his own thoughts and, by the nervous way he was twitching his riding crop against his thigh, I knew that he was annoyed by something. "Truly abominable procedure," he muttered under his breath. He cleared his throat and spoke aloud to me, "Letting one of the principals in the case see the testimony of the others before you have heard his story. The sworn statement puts one in mind of a person from the legal profession, does it not?"

"Edward Hewitt."

"Of course. Granted, it was probably too late by that time. Brother Edward must have spent many an hour by the sick-bed. Ah, well, it can't be undone. The police made a search along the road looking for another scene of violence. An utter waste of time."

"How is that?"

Holmes swept his hand along the scene before us: the bridge, the turning road and the treacherous slope. "Here is the scene of violence. Why should there have been two? The police would have done better to search every house between here and the village." Holmes could detect that

I was not following his train of thought. With a sigh, he paused to explain. "Isn't it the most logical that whoever had evil designs on Mrs Hewitt pursued her for some way down the road, until her wine-befuddled driver smashed the cart at the sharp turning here? With Collins seriously injured, how easy it must have been to overpower the lady. We don't know if she was injured when the cart overturned: I imagine she was. In fact, that would explain why the kidnappers never so much as sent their ransom note, if the lady had been fatally injured by the crash."

"Ransom, of course!" I exclaimed. "I never thought of that."

"Neither did the police, apparently. I consider it rather an odd omission in a case concerning the disappearance of a woman of wealthy family. Now, had the police been able to see their way to this utterly obvious idea, they would have also known in which direction to search for the abductors. What d'ye think about that, Watson? Had you kidnapped Mrs Hewitt, where would you go?"

At these moments in our association I was apt to feel like a schoolboy called upon to translate an unprepared passage of the Odes of Horace. But, as in the classroom, one might as well have a go at it. "I would not go back along the Bridgwater Road," I began, "because I would know that Colonel Hewitt might be riding from that direction at any moment. Assuming, that is, that if I were the kidnapper, I had written the note sending the Colonel to the ..ed Lion. And I wouldn't want to ride towards Coombehill, knowing that Mrs Hewitt has three grown sons who might be out looking for her. But Holmes, these are the only two directions from which to choose!"

"Not at all," smiled Holmes sardonically. "Get on your horse and follow me."

A quarter of a mile brought us to the junction of the Bridgwater and Quantock Roads. "Turn left, and approach East Quantock or right and ride the seven miles to Compton Green. Which shall it be?"

"What is in Compton Green?" I enquired.

"Little, but you wouldn't want to go that way." stated Holmes.

"Why not? I should want to go to the most deserted place I could find."

"Yes, but the Somerset Levels extend that way, and you would have to take the ferry at Berk's Crossing to get to your destination. Do you really want to have a conversation with the ferryman when you have an injured woman in the back of your cart?"

"Have I a cart?" I asked.

"If you have not, then you are carrying a dying woman across your saddle. Either way, I think you would avoid the ferryman."

"Very well, then, but dare I go to East Quantock?"

"Yes, Watson, I think you would. I think you might have had your hiding place prepared in advance, near the place where you expected to waylay Mrs Hewitt. I think you know the area and you know the Hewitt family. I think you would feel quite comfortable in going towards the village. Unless, of course, Coombehill is your home, in which case I believe you might be inclined to go in that direction, after all."

"Good heavens, Holmes," I gasped, "are you suggesting that one of the sons is the murderer?"

"David Hewitt is a possible candidate. Of all the family he had the weakest explanation for his movements that night. He claims he stayed in his room. A servant brought him tea in the late afternoon and another brought him something to eat at about nine o'clock, but, other than that, no one saw him. And yet, there is no evidence against his story either. No one saw him anywhere else about the house, in the grounds or along the roads, while the stablehands testified that he did not ask for a horse any time that evening. That is not to say that a determined man could not have found a way to provide himself with a horse or, for that matter, that he did not walk to the bridge, but I cannot help but feel that he would have had a more credible story ready for the police had he been part of a criminal plot."

I felt bound to indicate to Holmes that not every wrong-doer had his intelligence. "Perhaps it never occurred to him to create an alibi as he never thought that the police would doubt his story."

"And they have not doubted it, have they?" said Holmes with a wry smile.

A thought suddenly struck me. "What about the

similarity between the note given to Colonel Hewitt and that that David wrote to Jane Hewitt? Could that mean anything?"

Holmes half hooded his eyes in that familiar way of his. "Yes, I had considered that. It might mean something, but don't be too hasty to accuse just David. Both Andrew and Edward must also be included in your list of suspicious persons. You may think it unpalatable, but it is possible."

I bridled. "I will never believe that Andrew Hewitt could be involved in any such thing. You have despised him ever since you met him, in my opinion. You wanted to prove he had cut his own stirrup leather, as I recall."

"I did not want to prove it; I simply demonstrated how it might be done. In the same way, I merely point out that the two younger brothers very conveniently provide corroboration for each other's whereabouts at the crucial hours that evening."

"The servants must have served them supper and the stable boys must have saddled their horses," I said.

"That I grant you, but there are the hours before eight and after nine when we have only the words of Andrew and Edward as to their movements. And don't forget, only Edward actually made a statement to the police. Suppose that Collins had been acting as their agent, rather than their father's, as I hypothesised earlier. Suppose the younger brothers were plotting to hold their mother for ransom in order to drain some of the ready cash from the estate into their own pockets and suppose things went wrong, Collins driving the coach into the ditch and killing the woman. Edward and Andrew ride out to meet their co-conspirator and find their mother dead. Without the ransom they cannot afford to buy the groom's silence, so they kill him and conceal the mother's body to hamper any investigation. Andrew and Edward trust each other, but I doubt they had much faith in their accomplice, a known drunkard. Not to mention making a widow of the intriguing Mrs Collins."

"Holmes," I exclaimed, "of all your theories in this case, this is the most disgusting."

"I will tell you something for certain, if you prefer," said Holmes. "Edward Hewitt has been following us ever since we left the stables this afternoon."

THE DINNER

"Following us?" I repeated softly. I had already worked with Holmes long enough to know that when he informed me of such circumstances, I was not to cry out or dart looks in all directions. As for looking, I never supposed that I should be able to see anything that my eagle-eyed companion had missed.

"There seems to be something about us that intrigues Mister Edward, to be sure," said Holmes, while apparently gazing benignly at the landscape.

I murmured that we were being a little importunate regarding his family's affairs.

Holmes shrugged. "We are seeking justice, Watson. However, I mentioned Edward's presence for a particular reason. I have not objected to his company up to this point, but I would very much like to conduct the next phase of the investigation without him. I know you have some reservations about my methods in this case, Watson, but are you willing to assist me in ridding myself of him?"

Naturally, I agreed without demur.

"Good," said Holmes, producing his pocket watch. "It is rather late. Let us turn now and start back." When we had traversed a few hundred yards, Holmes turned to me again. "At some point I shall leave you on your own, Watson. Do not turn your head to look for me or for Mr Hewitt, for that matter. Keep your eyes to the front. You will not be in any danger. Go straight back to the stables and spend the rest of the afternoon in your room and maybe take forty winks. We may have a busy time ahead of us. I shall see you at supper, unless you have any questions to ask me now."

"You wouldn't answer the questions that I have," I grumbled.

Holmes chuckled quietly. I rode on, keeping my head straight ahead as he had asked. I believe that we parted company somewhere near the bridge, but he melted away so silently that I could not be sure. I only knew that I was suddenly aware that my horse's hooves alone were sounding within the tree-lined tunnel of the Bridgwater road. Let me tell you that it is an eerie feeling to know that someone may be following close behind you and not able to do even so much as glance in their direction. In spite of Holmes' expressed opinion that there was no danger, I was glad to see the inside of my room at Coombehill once more.

I took his advice and lay down to rest, though I doubted that I should sleep for thinking morbid thoughts about poor Elizabeth Hewitt being pursued to her death along that winding road at night, her only guardian the miserable drunken groom who had been the husband of auburn-haired Sally with the provoking, pouting lips that smiled at the mention of Andrew Hewitt's name. But I recognised that I was becoming drowsy when I began to imagine a flurry of secret notes scattered in all directions by a rampant red lion. I cannot recall the rest of my dreams, save that they had something to do with rats, kidnappers and dark, narrow lanes.

The noise of something falling nearby awakened me. As my head cleared I heard something lighter, a small article of furniture perhaps, hit the floor. The sounds were coming from just outside my door, so I went to it and peered outside into the corridor. The commotion was coming from Holmes' room and I heard his voice speaking in a low, but urgent, tone. In response came Andrew Hewitt's cry, "Fight fair, damn you!"

I quickly crossed the hall to see what the trouble might be. I found Andrew Hewitt struggling and protesting on the floor, attempting, with no success, to free himself from the grasp of Sherlock Holmes.

"Holmes!" I gasped. "What on earth is going on?"

"Watson," Holmes appeared unruffled despite the situation, "will you please explain to Mr Hewitt that he would do better not to engage me in a fist fight."

"Whatever did you do to provoke him?" I asked.

Neither of them would respond. Holmes merely snorted, while Hewitt choked out, "That is between us."

"Whatever it was, Hewitt," I said, "it is surely not worth risking your artistic career by breaking your knuckles on Holmes' chin."

"I don't care about my knuckles," said the man on the floor. "I simply want him to fight like a gentleman and take back what he said, instead of tripping me up and holding me down as if I were a child."

"I withdraw what I said," proffered Holmes. "I admit that I said it with the idea of provoking you, but I had hoped for words, not blows."

Hewitt seemed calmer, so my friend got to his feet and helped his erstwhile prisoner upright.

"If it will help to soothe your feelings," Holmes said pacifically, "please feel at liberty to throw whatever punches you like at me now."

Hewitt put up his fists and set his feet. Even I could see half a dozen flaws in his stance; the man was no pugilist. Beyond the novelty of his left-handedness, I doubted that Holmes would have the least trouble in parrying his attack. I knew Sherlock Holmes too well to suppose for a moment that he would stoop to retaliating against so inexperienced an opponent.

Holmes' relaxed posture confused the artist. "Well, sir, are you ready?"

Holmes smiled and appeared to relax even further.

"Then put up your guard, dammit."

"I prefer not to do so," replied Holmes.

"But I shall hit you easily if you won't defend yourself," spluttered Hewitt.

"No doubt you will," agreed Holmes.

Hewitt dropped his hands in exasperation. "I can't strike a man who won't put up his guard. You say you apologise? And you won't repeat what you said?"

"I regret saying it and I beg your pardon," said Holmes.

They shook hands briefly. Later on, when I told Hewitt what an expert boxer Holmes truly was, the artist had a hearty laugh about what he called his 'narrow escape from a bloody beating'. Hewitt was a decent fellow.

At that moment, however, he looked like a man in need of a drink, so I held out my flask to him. He took one gulp and was about to return the container to me when Holmes spoke, driving him to a second swallow.

"I do have another question or two for you, Mr Hewitt," was all he said.

"I tell you," said Hewitt defiantly, "I have done with talking about my mother. I don't believe I am obliged to answer any questions."

"No, you are not, but this concerns another member

of your family. I don't know if you realise how seriously Watson has been taking his responsibilities as your wife's cousin, but he tells me that he would like to hear the truth about your brother's broken engagement."

I protested my ignorance of this request, but Hewitt seemed too stunned by the mention of it to take any offence. His green eyes went wide and one hand distractedly pushed his rumpled hair back from his forehead. "My God," he murmured, "are you two magicians? Where did you hear of that?"

"From your brother David himself," answered Holmes.

"David," repeated Hewitt. He was still clearly shaken. "I thought it was all over and forgotten."

"Hardly, to hear your brother tell it. He seems quite bitter over your happiness and wants to spoil it if he can."

"You don't think he has told Jane, do you?" Andrew Hewitt asked anxiously.

"He told me to have her ask you about it," I assured him. "I don't believe that he has spoken to her." I thought of brother David's attempt to arrange a meeting with Jane Hewitt in the summer house and I recalled Dr Farthingale's story that David Hewitt's fiancée had been found in the very same location with Andrew. Had David planned to offer Jane more than money at their meeting? Had he some vile plan for history to repeat itself, but in reverse? It made me shudder to contemplate what might have happened had not her virtue and her good sense prevented her from keeping that appointment. A warning glance from Holmes reaffirmed my intention to say nothing to Andrew about his brother's note to his wife. The artist was mightily relieved simply to learn that his bride knew nothing of his own peccadillo.

"That's a blessing," said he. "If she must hear the story at all, I should prefer that she heard it from me. My part in it was far from admirable, but I am hardly the villain my brother supposed I was at the time. But how could I explain to him without causing further pain? I know he told you that I lured Helena to the summer house, but I never did. I'm not trying to say that I was blameless, but I insist that my fault was stupidity and nothing worse."

"Hewitt," I interposed, "there is really no reason for you to tell us this story. I am not your wife's cousin, and even if I were –"

"No, I want to tell you," declared Hewitt. "If I don't Mr Holmes will be sure that it is part of a grand conspiracy. It isn't a long story. Helena and I were chance partners in a treasure hunt. We always had parties and games in those days and guests by the dozen all summer long. As to the treasure hunt, you might imagine how useless I was when it came to puzzling out the clues. When Helena said that what we were looking for must be in the summer house, I supposed she had solved the clue. I sound even more idiotic than I was, but how can I explain? Ever since I was a little boy, the women and girls have always smiled at me: I supposed they smiled at every chap just the same. The world simply seemed to be a jolly place where everyone smiled at everyone else. Now I know better. But I tell you the truth that when we got to the summer house and Helena threw her arms around my neck – well, I was taken completely by surprise, and I had no idea how to get myself out of the situation I was in. As it happened a group of couples came upon us before I had quite thought of what it was I ought to do, one way or the other. And David, who was among the group, as ill luck would have it, found his fiancée there in my arms, in front of enough other witnesses to ensure his total and widespread humiliation. Poor David! But I thought he had forgiven me after all this time. You see why I couldn't tell him what I have told you. He thought Helena was a perfect goddess and wouldn't have believed me even had I tried to tell him she was not. Poor fellow!"

"And he has never married or shown interest in anyone else?" probed Holmes.

"No, David is really quite shy and reserved. He never would have become engaged to Helena except that she seemed determined to bring him out. Ned was of the opinion that she was a bit too forward. He supposed she had her eyes on David's birthright. I can answer for her being forward. Oh, I hate to think of poor David still tormenting himself over that fickle piece, when there are thousands of true-hearted girls just as lovely as she was. I dread telling this story to Jane, I can tell you."

"I shouldn't tell her, if I were you," I commented. "If your brother should mention it, that would be another thing, but for you to confess such a trivial incident to your wife would give it an importance it does not warrant. She might even see it as tasteless boasting on your part."

Holmes smiled. "Watson is an expert on such matters. Forgive me, Hewitt, I should not have inquired at all, were it not for the matter of Sally Collins."

"What about Sally Collins?" demanded the artist. There was no mistaking the note of apprehension in his voice.

"We happened to ride by Spring Green Cottage today," explained the detective.

"I doubt you have ever simply 'happened' to do anything in all your life, Mr Holmes. Why did you go there?"

"I was curious to see the woman who lives rent-free on your father's land and receives a tidy income besides."

"My family has always cared for the dependants of servants who have died or become unable to work," said Hewitt stiffly. "She is Jim Collins' widow and we do right by her. I trust you did not interrogate her about her bereavement."

"Oh, no," Holmes waved the suggestion aside. "We barely stayed long enough to introduce ourselves. She did ask us to wish you all happiness in your marriage, however." Holmes paused, then asked casually, "Do you ever visit her yourself?"

Andrew Hewitt drew himself up. "Why do you not just accuse me of being her lover straight away, Mr Holmes, so that I may deny it in no uncertain terms?"

"There is such a thing as protesting too much, Mr Hewitt," said Sherlock Holmes mildly.

"There is such a thing as prying too much, Mr Holmes," Andrew Hewitt retorted hotly. "For my part I don't care if you presume that I have seduced half the women in Somerset and Jane knows me too well to be hurt by gossip, but I'll tell you about Mrs Collins, just so that you will leave her out of your prurient imaginings. Her life has been troubled enough without that.

"She was not born to the serving class, her father owning a leather business in London, and her life would have been that of a gentlewoman had he not died when she was seventeen. She had met James Collins because he worked for her father and she had the misfortune to marry him before she truly knew his ways. He drank. He was apt to beat her when he drank. He quarrelled with the new owner of the business and lost his place there. He went on to humbler jobs, then lowly employment, and finally no work at all, save casual labour that he could pick up for a day or two. By this time they had an infant daughter to care for and were wandering from here to there, wherever he could find a crust.

"Then they came here and found my open-hearted mother, who was ready to tolerate the husband for the sake of the wife and child. You know what happened to Collins, but we have all of us continued to take an interest in his widow and her children. My mother would have wished it. And besides, Sally was very kind to me when I was ill. When she went to the village on market days she would call in at Dr Farthingale's and stay the afternoon, baking special treats for me to try to entice me to eat. I would play with the children: it's hard to be quite so sad in the presence of little children. The girl can draw rather well and the boy wants to learn to ride well enough someday so that I will let him up on Grenadier. Ned and I are planning - but all this is very boring to you, isn't it, Mr Holmes? There is no murder or scandal in it. Are you satisfied? Will you leave Mrs Collins alone?"

Holmes shrugged. "As you wish."

"That's better then," said Hewitt briskly. "I so hate quarrelling with you, Mr Holmes. I can hardly stay angry at a chap who has praised my work, you know. Please try to forget your investigations and just enjoy yourself here. We'll give you something to chase tomorrow, I hope. Let a rascally fox be your quarry. But now I must go and make arrangements for our supper. I know it isn't essential now that we know I'm not about to be murdered, but I am going to tell my father about my marriage tonight, come what may. Wish me luck!"

"Good luck!" I called as he darted out of the door. By the time I turned around, Holmes had flung himself upon the bed and was staring at the ceiling above. "You will leave the woman alone, as you promised, won't you, Holmes?" I asked.

"Of course. You don't imagine that her story would differ from his in the least degree, do you?" he snapped.

"Can't you take the word of a gentleman?" I demanded

with some heat.

"Oh, Watson, please," Holmes sighed. "I have had enough of these public school heroics. As a matter of fact, I do believe him. It's a pity."

"How is it a pity?"

"He has explained the reason she stays on here, and the reason that he visits her, but has left out one important point in her story."

"And what is that," I enquired.

"I don't understand why the nomadic Collins entourage wandered all the way from London to the West Country to find a situation for the husband on this estate."

"Well," I offered, somewhat weakly, I admit, "they simply did, that is all."

"Watson, for two generations and more, the population of the English countryside have been moving away from their farms and their little villages to find work in the cities and the larger towns. To find work in the factories and on the docks, in the shops and in the banks. The working men go where work is to be found, my friend. If a man goes swimming against such a tide, I consider he has a reason."

"Perhaps Hewitt might have told you had you asked."

"Maybe. But he assumes we are satisfied now and such a question..." Here he drifted into some channel of thought which he did not wish to share with me. All at once he sprang to his feet and I supposed he had some clue for us to follow. Instead, he turned to me with an exaggerated look of consternation on his face. "Watson, we cannot appear at the dinner table in this shabby condition. Off you go to your tub and I to mine."

§§§

My next glimpse of my friend was at the dinner table that evening when we all sat down to another grand meal. From his clouded looks, I gathered that his mood had deteriorated during the intervening time, perhaps due to some check in the progress of his theories. On the other hand, Andrew Hewitt was on the point of bursting with high spirits. He had a smile and a pleasant word for each of us, with special beaming smiles towards his wife, who could not help but reflect his every sunny glance. He had evidently decided to postpone his announcement until after the meal and, considering what followed, it was just as well we had our nourishment to fortify us.

As we were finishing our dessert, the servants entered with champagne and glasses for the company. While his father looked stern and puzzled, Andrew Hewitt rose to his feet.

"If I may have your attention," he began, somewhat unnecessarily, since we were all staring at him, "I should like to tell you all something that it is past time you knew. Jane, my dearest, please stand beside me. Gentlemen, I am proud to tell you that on the tenth of March at St Cedd's, Westminster, this beautiful lady became my wife. I have loved her since I first saw her and shall love her until the last breath leaves my body. Will you please raise your glasses with me and drink her health."

Edward Hewitt was the first on his feet with his glass in hand. A moment later only the Colonel and his eldest son were still in their chairs.

Then the old soldier rose slowly. "How like you it is to have handled the matter in such an awkward way," he said. "I might have expected that you would have rushed into the thing without much time for reflection. And yet –" He turned to the couple and his warlike face softened at the handsome sight they made together. "May God bless you both," he finished quickly.

David Hewitt kept his seat and glared at the rest of us as we toasted the young couple and their union. When he finally stood, I had hopes that he was prepared to offer some good wishes of his own, but his bitterness clearly ran too deep for that. Instead, he carried his glass across to his mother's portrait, where he paused, as if to contemplate her lovely face. Then he looked over his shoulder at us. "Let us drink to love and constancy," he said with a sneering smile. "And to our mother, wherever she may be tonight."

Andrew Hewitt dropped his glass and, but for his wife's restraining arms, would surely have crossed the room to challenge his brother there and then. In the delay while he sought to disengage her grasp, the colonel joined his eldest before the painting.

"Now is not the time for this, David. If you cannot join in wishing your own brother happiness, I suggest you leave the company for the time being."

"Why should I wish him the very thing that he has stolen from me?" flashed David Hewitt. "I'll do some harm to everyone before I go. I have something to show you, Father. You might find it rather interesting."

From his pocket he drew a small pocket notebook, the very one that Heywood Melrose had used to jot down his information for Sherlock Holmes, and proffered it to his father. I tried to catch my friend's eye across the table, but he was engrossed in the scene before us.

"Open it. Do," urged David. "See on this page, and this. It is a tidy summary of your assets and liabilities. What were you about, Melrose, adding up the worth of the Hewitt estate? I wonder you bother. There are three healthy lives between it and your clever niece. Go ahead, why don't you try to deny that this book belongs to you."

"Melrose!" cried Colonel Hewitt. "Is this truly your notebook and your writing?"

"It does appear to be," said Melrose mildly, "but how it came from my room into Mr Hewitt's hands, I cannot imagine."

"You dropped it on the staircase, you old fool," jeered David.

"That is simply impossible," protested Melrose. "I packed that notebook in my bag for safe keeping."

Colonel Hewitt tore the offending pages from the book and tossed the mutilated volume at Melrose's feet. "You may pack it once again, sir. You leave my house tomorrow. Don't deny that you went into my private study to satisfy your greedy curiosity concerning my business affairs. Perhaps you might explain how you were able to get in; I never fail to lock the door behind me."

"I assure you that I had only the highest motives for doing so," insisted Melrose, with reddening face. I must say that the man rose in my estimation during this exchange. Neither by word nor look did he betray his connection with Sherlock Holmes.

Now Holmes stepped forward to retrieve the fallen notebook and, passing it to Melrose, he calmed him with a gesture indicating his willingness to carry the burden of the argument from thence on. Melrose sat down.

"It was I who opened the door of your study," Holmes

announced quietly. "Mr Melrose went through your papers at my request."

"At your request, sir?" The old soldier stepped face to face with the detective, his grey moustache bristling. "Who are you, Mr Sherlock Holmes? And what are you doing under my roof after all?"

"I am a searcher after truth," replied Holmes enigmatically.

"The truth about my financial situation, sir?"

"The truth is not limited to a single aspect of a man's life. It extends in all directions, wherever his actions affect the lives of others."

The Colonel was not assuaged. "Say what you mean, dammit. Who are you, I say? What are you?"

"I am a private consulting detective," said Holmes.

"A detective! We have no need for detectives here." Suddenly the old man turned on his youngest son. "It's your doing, of course. You never will let it rest, will you? Was this Farthingale's latest notion? A detective? Speak up, you miserable excuse for a son of mine."

Andrew slowly rose from his seat. "It isn't what you think, Papa," he said hopelessly. "Dr Farthingale had nothing to do with it. Mr Holmes is here because I asked him to come and investigate my recent fall."

"Poppycock! What is there to investigate about a fall from a horse?"

Andrew paled, but persisted. "I fell because of a flaw in the saddle. I wanted Mr Holmes to determine if that flaw was accidental or contrived."

"Contrived, by heaven! Contrived by whom?"

"By no one, as it turns out," Andrew waved his hands apologetically. "Mr Holmes has demonstrated that beyond the shadow of a doubt."

"I fail to see what my accounts have do do with that matter," bellowed the Colonel.

"Clearly nothing, but how was Mr Holmes to know that until he had all of his evidence?" Andrew seemed desperate before his father's outrage.

"This is arrant nonsense, that's what it is. Can you give me no better lie than this? Leave the lying to Holmes, why don't you? He is a splendid man with a lie. Or Dr Watson, who I must say had me completely taken in."

Andrew made a last attempt to pacify his parent. "Papa, listen to me –"

"In my household, you listen to me. I shall say this only once, before I order the whole pack of you out. I know very well what you are about with your detectives and your plots. I thought perhaps you had given up trying to destroy me with your accusations about your mother, but I see now you have not. Your fall was nothing but a convenient excuse to call in outside help. Well, you are doomed to fail as you failed three years ago. I had witnesses to my whereabouts all that evening. Go and ask Superintendent Bellows where I was that night, if your own father's word is not sufficient for you."

Two open-mouthed servants who had come in to clear away our dishes scurried out again in amazement and terror as the father aimed a blow at the son, who parried the hit. We all joined in to restrain the would-be combatants: Edward and David tending to their father, while Holmes and I held back Andrew, impeded though we were by his wife's well-meaning efforts to calm him. Only Heywood Melrose kept apart, his elbows on the table and his face in his hands.

We were able to separate them before any blows fell, but it was impossible to silence them. It was regrettable that a lady was present at their heated exchange, but no more regrettable than that any two men so close in blood should be capable of accusing each other of such things. At length their mutual fury had run its course, and the Colonel nodded to his sons that he wished to be released from their grasp.

"I am going to leave this room now," he said, dusting himself down. "I require that you all leave my house without my seeing you again. The first train in the morning will do."

"I'll go after I've ridden in the hunt," retorted his youngest son.

"Do as you wish, sir, but keep out of my sight. And when you go take your red horse with you, if you please. If he spends another night in my barn, I'll butcher him and feed him to Vickers' hounds."

The old warrior retired from the field of battle, his elder sons in attendance. We released our charge when they were completely out of sight. A moment later, Edward Hewitt reappeared in the doorway and beckoned to his younger brother.

"Andrew, what have you done?" the barrister asked.

Andrew Hewitt answered with a shake of his head and a helpless wave of his hands.

"It would be better if you would leave, as Papa said. I'll see what I can do once you and the others are out of the way."

The younger man found his voice, "I want to talk to you and Papa before I go. I have some questions."

"I'm not sure that I trust you any more, Andrew, but I'll hear you out in the morning if you are determined to stay and cause more trouble."

Edward Hewitt turned and left the room, leaving Andrew standing with bowed shoulders at the door. He shook his head and, pulling himself together, hurried across to embrace his wife. "I'm so sorry," we heard him say. "It has all gone so wrong." Her response was inaudible to us, but seemed to give him some consolation, for he turned to us with admirable self-control. "My wife and I are going upstairs now. If I don't see you again, Mr Holmes, Dr Watson, thank you coming all this way to try to help us. You did your job well; it's only a shame that my brother found that notebook."

All of us took our cue to retire as well, except for Holmes, who followed me to my room, perching himself upon my open window sill to smoke a cigarette.

"Have a care, Holmes," I warned, "you'll fall through."

He waved his hand either to assure me that his seat was secure or to indicate that he did not care if he were to fall or not.

"I'm sorry this case has ended in frustration for you," I ventured. "But you did, at least, solve the mystery of the stirrup leather."

"That was nothing," Holmes mused aloud. "All this annoys me because I know that at the bottom of his heart Andrew Hewitt wishes me to find out what happened to his mother. Without his co-operation, I must take the long way to the truth. And yet, I would have thought that tonight's confrontation with his father would have done the trick."

"What trick?" Holmes talks in riddles sometimes.

"I had hoped that a rousing argument with his parent would have decided our young friend once and for all in favour of a full investigation into the family secrets. Otherwise I never should have caused poor Melrose such embarrassment with his notebook."

"That was hardly your fault," I said. "David was to blame for that."

"Yes, but I'm afraid that it was I who took the notebook from Melrose's bag and left it on the staircase where Mister David was sure to find it."

I was flabbergasted. "What a terrible thing to do."

"I gambled and lost," said he with a shrug of his shoulders.

"You gambled," I said with emphasis, "and that dear young couple lost. How could you do such a thing, Holmes? Did you see how happy Andrew Hewitt was when his father gave his blessing to the marriage? The family was close to reconciliation and you destroyed it all because of your infernal curiosity."

Holmes had the grace to look shame-faced, but riposted, "Well, it was too late by then. David Hewitt already had the notebook in his pocket. You know, I believe there is that in the Somerset air that makes men contentious. Two days breathing it has made you much more argumentative than you are apt to be in London."

"I cannot help but think it is none of our affair." So saying I sat down and folded my arms, wishing to imply that the discussion was at an end.

Holmes, however, did not give up so easily. "If she is dead, it is every man's affair. Do you not wish to see justice done, Watson?"

"By all means," I acknowledged, "but with the trail three years old, you are doomed to failure."

"I don't know that yet," said Holmes. "It would have been easier with the help of the Hewitts. Who can tell what they know? I was a fool to be pushed on to that old doctor, who told us the truth as far as it went, but left out much that might have been helpful. Andrew Hewitt knows something that he will not tell - you heard him say so. He is protecting someone else." Holmes ground out the stub of his cigarette on the window sill and got to his feet. "I'll speak to Andrew once more in the morning. You may let me know your own plans at that time."

§§§

But our plans were to be determined by yet one more event that night. I had prepared for bed after Holmes' departure, but found I could not sleep for mulling over the evening's drama, both the debacle at the supper table and my disagreement with Holmes over his tactics in the case. For an hour or more I lay awake in the darkness.

Then a soft knock on my door brought me to my feet in an instant. I made my way across the black room and pulled the knob towards me, wondering what member of the household would come calling at this late hour when all the house was so quiet. Behind a wavering candle flame I could discern the tall figure and tousled hair of Andrew Hewitt. He wavered like his candle and the reek of liquor was strong as he passed me on his way into my room.

"I am sorry to disturb you, cousin," he began, his usually bright voice slurred and weary. "Is it all right or shall I go?"

"Of course it is all right. Sit down, you look terrible."

"No, I won't sit," said he, albeit clutching at the foot of my bed to steady himself. "The truth is I want to see Mr Holmes, but was afraid to go in by myself. Will you come with me? Is there any chance he'll still be ready to help me or is he too angry with me?"

"We'll go and see him together," I reassured him. "Let me have that candle; you'll set the house afire." I was not that certain Holmes would wish to see the man in this condition, but if Hewitt would not speak when he was sober, perhaps Holmes would have to take him as he was. Either way, it was not my place to stand between Sherlock Holmes and people who were seeking his aid, so I threw on my dressing-gown and led Hewitt, stumbling, across the hall to my friend's room.

THE DISAPPEARANCE

It was not necessary to wake Holmes either. Though he was in his dressing gown and the room was dark save for the fire-light, we found him alert in his chair, a glowing pipe between his teeth. At the sight of us, he rose, took up the poker and stirred the embers back to life. In the red and shifting light, his eyes took on a weird sort of glitter, as if they too were about to kindle into flame. The sight of him seemed to give our client something of a fright and he staggered back against my arm.

"I - I suppose it's not too late to tell you my story?" he faltered in a quavering voice.

Holmes looked askance at Hewitt's condition, but he took him by the arm in a comradely way and led him to the chair by the fire. "Not at all," he assured the artist in his most soothing tone. "Here; sit here."

"May I ask you something first, Mr Holmes? Before I say anything else? I want to know if it would be possible - that is, if you can tell me what happened to my mother - if it would be possible for you to simply tell me what you decide is the truth and allow me to pursue such course of action as I should then think proper?"

"Meaning that I should take no further action?" said Holmes.

"Yes. You aren't the police, after all."

"I may not be the official arm of the law," said Holmes slowly, "but I have my own conscience and code of conduct. I cannot in good faith promise you what I might or might not feel compelled to do once we learn the truth."

"You mean, Once I set you on, I cannot call you off?"

"I am not one of the Master's hounds," replied Holmes with a smile. "I must always act as I think best. That is the only condition under which I agree to help you. However, you may find that I keep a greater store of sympathy and understanding than you might suppose. Do you imagine that a perfectly decent fellow like Watson would stay in my company for five minutes if he did not know that I temper my justice with mercy?"

Hewitt looked at me and seemed reassured by my nod. "I don't know what else to do, then," he said. "I shall have to put my trust in you. I am prepared to tell you everything that concerns myself and my mother, but there is one matter I cannot reveal. I swear it has nothing to to do with my mother's death. Will you still help me, even though I must hold this back from you? I am going as far as I dare even to speak to you. I had hoped you might solve the mystery without my having to tell you anything."

"I know you did," Holmes said. "I followed up every hint that you let fall, but they have come to nothing when so much has been concealed. Even your full story may not be enough to solve it, do you understand?"

"Jane warned me of that," Hewitt said in a low tone. "I talked it over with her before I came to see you tonight. She thinks I must tell you my story in any case – that I could never be quite easy with myself again if I let this chance slip by. She understands that the only reason I agreed to let her uncle send for you was because I secretly hoped you would solve all of our mysteries."

"Very well then," said Holmes, patting the artist's arm reassuringly. "I want you to tell me about the last time you saw your mother. Think back to that day... Don't be worried if the events seem very ordinary."

I took a seat on Holmes' bed, anticipating a long night. Hewitt was momentarily silent with the effort of recalling the past, but he seemed more resolute now. When he lifted his face to Holmes all traces of fear and doubt were gone. He seemed a touch more sober, though his slurring speech betrayed him now and again.

"It was certainly an ordinary enough day at the start. Breakfast... riding... tea. Mother attended to her correspondence, gave instructions to the servants about the meals, that sort of thing."

Holmes interrupted. "This correspondence. Do you know who received these letters from your mother?"

"My aunt – her sister – was one. I know because she spoke to me later about how cheerful the letter was. How no one would ever have supposed anything was amiss. Meanwhile my father was in a black mood; that was less usual in those days than it is now. I remember feeling relieved that at least it couldn't have been over anything I had done, as we had not been in dispute recently. I couldn't imagine what was the matter with him at the time, but now I see he must have already found that note."

"We'll get back to that later," said Holmes. "What time did your mother leave to visit her sick neighbour?"

"Let's see," I could observe the racking of the memory going on, "we had luncheon at two, so she could not have left before three. Sometime after three, it must have been; but not long after. I wish I could be more precise."

"You are doing very well," encouraged Holmes. "Can you recall what she took with her on this visit?"

"Oh, heavens, I helped her with the bundles myself. Let me think. Yes, there were some jars: honey and jam, I think. I remember honey for certain, because I'm rather fond of honey myself. I couldn't resist having a look in the basket, because it was so heavy for its size. There were the pots and there were a couple of books. It was a three-volume novel, but I can't recall the title, I'm afraid. The jars were covered with a cloth to keep them apart from the books, but there was hardly room for anything larger than a couple of handkerchiefs at most."

"And there was no other luggage in the rear of the cart?" Holmes probed.

"I can't say that I looked, but I suppose that had there been something, I would have noticed it because it would have been strange."

"Do you remember if your mother sat in the back herself or did she take the seat next to the driver?"

"Without doubt she was up with the driver. She would have wanted to talk to him, because my mother talked to everyone, always. The idea of riding silently along with a fellow human being nearby would never have occurred to her. My mother was half Irish, you know, and could she talk! No, Mr Holmes, not in the way you think. She had the gift of recounting the simplest happenings in life with such wit and such wonderful good humour that it was always a delight to be with her. She had a knack of drawing out the other person in the kindest way. She had so much love in her soul that it could not help but shine through in everything she —" Hewitt pulled a kerchief from his pocket and mopped his eyes.

"In any case Collins worshipped my mother. She was very kind to him and he appreciated what she had done for him. She knew, for example, how he hated the routine of the stable work, so she made a point of asking for him as her driver whenever she went shopping or to pay her calls. Compared to mucking out the stalls, driving around the countryside in a cart has much to commend it."

"Did Collins think that you and his wife were lovers?" asked Holmes.

"Good heavens, no! It wasn't so."

"Forgive me, Mr Hewitt." Holmes had rarely sounded less penitent. "I am prepared to accept your word that you were not her lover, but in her husband's eyes even an innocent relationship might have been less than welcome."

"I wouldn't have said that she and I truly became friends until after he was dead," said Hewitt, appreciably more sober now. "It isn't possible to maintain a genuine friendship with one of the servants. She and I happened to chat from time to time when she was working in the kitchen and I happened to find my way there to steal a few treats from the oven. But there were generally other servants about and I spoke to them as well. I like the company of women, I suppose. Collins resented me as he resented all the men in the house, simply because he hated being a servant. He had once been a man of business and it hurt his pride to have fallen so low."

"So neither your mother nor the groom showed any signs of anxiety that day?"

"Not that I was aware. My mother kissed me good-bye as she always did, and she told me she would see me at supper at eight."

"And what did you do for the remainder of the day?"

"I went to my room to continue painting. I took tea later; Ned joined me."

"Was that usual?" asked Holmes.

"Oh, yes. It bores Ned to watch me paint, but he would pop in and out to see how I was getting on. And just so that we could chat together. He had a couple of slack days in his law practice, and with the hunting and shooting in the autumn Ned liked to be home as much as possible. After that night he stayed on for two more weeks, until the house was back to some sort of normal state."

"You are rushing your fences again, Mr Hewitt," Holmes reproved. "Did you go on painting until supper-time?"

"Yes, I was working well and lost all track of time. Ned came to fetch me, saying that no one else was on time for dinner and that I had to come to keep him company."

"Where was everyone else?" enquired Holmes.

"Father had gone out: he'd told Ned he was going to Fenny Burton to meet a man about some horses. I didn't know where David was, but it turned out that he'd decided to stay in his room that evening. That sort of thing often happened with David, so we were not concerned."

"And you thought you knew where your mother was," stated Holmes. "At what time in the evening did you become concerned about her?"

"When we had finished supper and she still had not returned, I thought it would do no harm to ride towards the Dudleys and see if she needed anything. So I started about nine o'clock; I confess I hurried through my supper because I was a little worried. It was not like her to stay past her time anywhere without sending us word."

"So you started off for Primrose Hill at just past nine. It's just short of four miles from here, I gather."

Hewitt nodded.

"Tell me what you found," continued Holmes, "when you rode along the way to the Dudleys. Edward went with you, as I believe you have already said."

"Yes. I don't know if you are familiar with the spot, but we found the overturned cart just at the place where the road bends at a sharp angle on this side of the stone bridge. It was on its side just off the highway and the horse was still hitched to it. The harness had not broken, though everything was twisted and the horse couldn't move a step from where he was."

"In what direction was the horse facing?" asked Holmes.

"In the direction of Coombehill, as you would expect."

Holmes smiled and shook his head. "What we would expect and what actually happened are often quite different. Please go on. What did you do?"

"We dismounted at once. Naturally we were horrified, because we expected to find mother injured - but we didn't find her, of course. We discovered only Collins, lying just downhill from the cart. He was unconscious, but he was breathing."

"How was he breathing? Normally or rapidly?"

"I'm afraid we paid very little attention to Collins. We went on searching for our mother. There was a lantern on the cart; it had gone out, but we lit it again and searched with it. It became obvious that she was not there and, at the time, Ned and I thanked God for that, as we assumed she must have changed her mind and decided to spend the night at Primrose Hill. It made sense, you see; she had sent Collins back with the message, and he had run himself off the road. Well, once we were satisfied she was in no danger, we had a little more thought to spare for Collins. We tried to bring him round, but we got no response at all from him. We could smell the wine on his breath, naturally, but he wasn't drunk or I think we could have roused him a little. Ned decided we should fetch Dr Farthingale out. I had the quicker horse, so I rode to the village while Ned stayed with Collins."

"So you continued across the bridge and turned left at the crossroads a quarter of a mile from there?"

Hewitt shot Holmes an admiring glance. "You have certainly learnt the lie of the land, Mr Holmes. Yes, that is the quickest way to town from the bridge."

"At what time would you say you started for the doctor?" pressed Holmes.

"It must have been a little after ten by that time. I didn't look," admitted Hewitt. "But I was in Dr Farthingale's parlour by half past ten. I remember the clock over the mantle."

"That was a brisk ride in the dark of night," commented Holmes.

"I know the roads, and so does Grenadier. And the doctor's cottage is on the near side of the village to us."

"Had the doctor already retired for the night when you knocked on his door?"

"No, I saw a light in his bedroom window. And he came straight to the door when I knocked, though he was in his night-gown and did look a little drowsy. Since his wife's death, he had got into the habit of taking a drink or two to help him get to sleep at night. I had the impression that I had caught him in between the drink and his sleep. I told him what had happened and asked him to come."

"Did he say anything you can recall?"

"Yes, he said - and I remember this distinctly because it became important later on - he said, 'Thank heavens your mother decided to stay the night at Primrose Hill.' He had been there earlier himself and had talked to mother. She happened to mention to him that she intended to stay there. At the time, he offered to go the long way home and leave a message with us at Coombehill, but mother wouldn't hear of troubling him, and she said she would send word back by Collins."

"Did anyone find a note on Collins' person?"

"No," said Hewitt, a worried frown on his forehead, "but, you see, she couldn't have been planning to stay with the Dudleys. She left in the cart with Collins after all. At least three servants there saw her go."

"But at the time you went to fetch the doctor you had no way of knowing that and therefore you and he had no worries about Mrs Hewitt."

"None, until we reached the bridge once again. My father was there, having ridden home from Fenny Burton by way of Primrose Hill. He knew for certain that mother was not there or anywhere along the road leading from there. Then we truly began to worry. And worst of all, Collins had died. The only person who might have given us any clue as to what really happened."

"He was alive, but unconscious, when you left for Dr Farthingale's?"

"As I said," said Hewitt, with a touch of acerbity, "although he seemed in a pretty bad way. I really wasn't all that surprised to find that he was dead. His breathing had been simply awful. Oh, yes. You asked me about his breathing, didn't you? It was more like gasping. And we were not able to get a word out of him. He had died without a word to Ned, who had stayed by him the entire time. I'm sure that Ned did all he could, though he isn't qualified to help a man in the plight that Collins seemed to be."

Holmes might have been a barrister, like Edward Hewitt, in the way he posed probing question after probing question. "Did Collins die before or after your father arrived? That is, was your brother perhaps distracted briefly upon your father's unexpected arrival, so that he might have been less attentive to the dying man?"

"I couldn't say," admitted Hewitt, "but he always insisted that he had watched Collins the entire time, and that he had died without coming round."

"What did the four of you do then, when you realised that something was seriously amiss with Mrs Hewitt?"

"I'm afraid my father acted rather badly. He said some quite outrageous things to Dr Farthingale."

"With reference to the doctor's love for Mrs Hewitt, I presume. There is no need to stare at me in such amazement. It is a matter of police record that your father had unpleasant things to say about the doctor and about you. As for the doctor's being infatuated with your mother, that seems to have been common knowledge."

"Common gossip, you mean!" Hewitt was affronted. "No man will allow that a man and a woman can simply be fast friends. And why ever not, I ask you? They were friends and nothing more. I would have known it. I knew them both far better than any of the people who fed you those lies. It was a beautiful, tender friendship, but it was nothing beyond that!"

"I take it," said Holmes mildly, "that you defended your friend the doctor with equal fervour that night on the road, which only infuriated your father further?"

"He was not pleased with me, but Ned managed to head him off by getting us all to think about what we must do next. About Collins, about finding mother. My father calmed down a bit and we loaded Collins into the gig - Dr Hugh confirmed that he was dead - so that the doctor could take him back to Coombehill. My father said that the three of us were going to make a search of the road from the bridge back to Primrose Hill, but in truth we did no such thing. Instead, he showed me a piece of paper and demanded to know what I knew of it. It was a note, Mr Holmes, asking my mother to meet the writer at a pub in Fenny Burton. My father seemed convinced that I -"

"Wait a moment!" interrupted Holmes imperiously. "The note was unsigned?"

Hewitt hesitated for a fraction before replying, "I don't recall a signature of any kind."

"Can you remember how the note was worded?" Holmes persisted. "I know three years have passed, but every detail is of importance. The paper itself - could you see what it was? Was it a leaf from a notebook, for example?"

"Oh dear, I can't recall." I could see that young Hewitt was racking his brains in an effort to remember. "I think it was ordinary note-paper. Nothing remarkable about it that I can recall. I saw it only the once by lantern-light and father was rather waving it about, of course."

"What was the exact, I repeat exact, wording? Can you concentrate?" Holmes was looking intently at our client, as if willing him to retrieve every scrap of information from his memory.

"I don't think I can recall," Hewitt faltered. "It began 'My dearest Bess', I do remember that much. And it mentioned Tuesday night. I forget the time. The writer was making an appointment with her at the *Red Lion* and he wanted to get a couple of hours start, something like that. I was so stunned by what it said. I couldn't make sense of it, because I knew perfectly well that mother had gone to see Mrs Dudley."

"Was it in pen or pencil?"

"I can't remember." His inability to recall the details of the note was making Hewitt very anxious, but Holmes pressed on relentlessly.

"Was it long-hand or printed?"

"Printed, I think. I'm not sure."

"Come, Hewitt, make an effort," urged Holmes irritably.

"I am doing my best." Hewitt had begun to rock forward and back in his seat like a nervous child and his hands constantly worried his dark hair. Clearly Holmes' badgering was taking its toll on his mental state. For my part, I could not understand why it was necessary to subject our sensitive client to such torment, when Holmes had seen the note for himself that very morning.

In my own agitation and concern for Andrew Hewitt, I must have made a discernable sound, for Holmes raised his hand as a sign that I should not interrupt the proceedings. I might have interfered against his wishes, had not my friend himself begun to show an inclination to be more gentle. He did no more than place his hand on the young artist's shoulder, but it was enough to stop Hewitt from his twitching and swaying. It struck me then, seeing them both in profile against the firelight, how these two men who were so close in age seemed each composed of the parts the other lacked: Holmes, all determination, strength and reason, and Hewitt, beauty, emotion and vulnerability. Yet each had in common a strong creative spark and a certain courage too, and something else not easily put into words: something that seemed to draw them irresistibly to each other, if not in accord, then in conflict. Whatever it was, it was responsible for their mutual determination to find the truth in this case which was giving so much frustration to the one and so much sorrow to the other.

"I know it is difficult after all this time," continued Holmes in a softer tone. "Is there anything else at all that you can tell me about the note?"

"I'm afraid there isn't. If only I hadn't been so upset. I was all right until I found that mother was really missing and, after that, everything is a blur of my father's shouting and my own confusion."

"I do understand. Would some brandy help now? Watson, if you please."

Hewitt drank the brandy I brought him in a single gulp that made him gasp and dab his eyes with his handkerchief. "Let's get this over with," he said with a rueful grin.

"Right," said Holmes, reverting to his usual brisk manner. "Now, don't be upset if you cannot remember everything. Most of all I want your impressions of that night and what you were thinking at the time. For example, did it seem to you that your father had his own ideas as to who had written that note to your mother?"

"Yes, I think he wanted me to say that it was from Dr Farthingale. But why should he arrange a secret rendezvous with my mother when he could drive up to Coombehill any day of the week and see her? I mean, even if you believe the worst of them, surely it would have been easier for them simply to pick any time that we were all out riding. Why go to all that trouble?"

"And to the best of your knowledge, Dr Farthingale and your mother had no plans to run away together?"

"That is a ridiculous idea. Anyway, the doctor is still here and my mother is gone."

"Then you are quite sure that Farthingale was not the author of the note." Holmes leant back in his chair.

"Quite sure," affirmed Hewitt. "He is a dear old fellow with nothing but goodness in his heart. You may take the word of someone who has known him twenty-nine years."

"Your father was convinced you did know who had written the note. Did you write it yourself?"

Hewitt shot bolt upright. "No, I did not!"

"The question had to be asked." Holmes tried to pacify our client. "You are sure that you did not see it until that night when your father showed it? Think carefully. Could the memory of it have been lost following your injury?"

"Is that possible?" asked the artist, his eyes troubled. He slumped back in his chair, his face towards the fire. After a moment he returned from his meditations with a shake of the head. "It's true," he murmured, "I've lost some hours and days - even a week here and there - after I struck my head. And everything is foggy after the shock of discovering that mother was gone. But I feel quite sure of what I did up to that time, Mr Holmes. If I had had anything to do with some plot, I should remember."

Holmes seemed satisfied with this and abandoned his questions about the note. "Tell me, are there any other inns or ale-houses nearby called the *Red Lion*, besides that in Fenny Burton?"

"The next nearest that I know of is in Colewood - and that is fifteen miles from here and not close to anything. Whereas Fenny Burton is only five miles from Taunton and the Great Western Railway."

Holmes accepted this statement without comment and appeared to change the course of the interrogation again. "Tonight at the dinner table you accused your father of being responsible for your mother's death. Do you truly believe he was responsible?"

"Of course not," said Hewitt stoutly. "I only said it to make him angry. It never fails to make him angry. I said the same thing that first night. I did not know at the time where he had been or that other people had seen him. Mother was gone and he was shouting absolute nonsense to me about notes and Dr Farthingale. I don't know that I believed what I was saying even then, but it popped into my head and out it came before I considered whether it was true or not."

"What did he do when you first accused him of killing your mother?" asked Holmes.

"He struck me with all his might. I wasn't prepared and I went staggering back. I tripped and hit the back of my head on something. You both saw the scar. Not that I had any idea what happened at the time. The last thing I remember is my brother's voice, shouting, 'Papa, don't!' I woke in my room with my head simply roaring and Ned bending over me."

"Does anyone else know the truth about your injury besides your father and your brother, Edward?"

"I told Jane, but I swore her to secrecy about it. That's the reason she was so desperate to have you down to find out about the stirrup leather. She doesn't know father and she was frightened that he was trying to injure me again. I tried to explain that he wouldn't, but who could blame her for not being able to understand my family."

Holmes smiled. "I confess I don't understand them either. In particular, I cannot see why your father was so firmly convinced that his wife left him, when everyone who speaks of her insists that she was incapable of doing such a thing."

Hewitt was by now almost sober and he said quietly, "Possibly his conscience troubled him for the way he treated her. He wasn't violent, but there is a cruel streak in him, a wish to dominate others, to stifle their nature and bend them to his will. I don't know what he thought gave him the right. After all, who asked him to leave his precious regiment and all those bloody wars he was so good at? My mother, of course, was glad when he came home to stay; she adored him. She fell in love with him when she was sixteen and he was a dashing ensign. And he is a great man, there is no denying it; a brilliant soldier, an excellent landlord."

"But a bad father?" interposed Holmes.

"Not at all. He could be wonderful at times. When he was showing me how to ride and shoot, when I could please him at those things. He had ambitions for me to turn into a recruit for a regiment of horse, but mother and I banded together to defy him secretly. I'd have been in India today had it not been for her encouragement and strength."

"Perhaps your father was jealous of your affinity with your mother?" Holmes suggested. "When she vanished, both were predisposed to think the worst of the other."

Hewitt looked uncomfortable and growled, "It might have been something like that."

"Tell me about your recovery from your injury." Again Holmes appeared to change the subject. "I don't understand why you were taken to Dr Farthingale's, rather than allowed to recuperate at home."

"That is simple. Father could not bear the sight of me. Ned thought it would be better if I went away and Doctor Hugh was kind enough to take me in."

"That is strange," demurred Holmes, "I received the impression that your brother does not think very highly of Dr Farthingale."

"But he is fond of me and I was seriously ill. Where better than a doctor's? I found it hard to remember things. I could recognise people, you see, but sometimes it was a struggle to think of their names."

"In your condition," prompted the detective, "there would have been a lapse of time before you were capable of understanding the conclusions that the police had drawn about your mother's disappearance."

"Even a man with a clear head would have had trouble understanding how they could have left the case as it was," said Hewitt bitterly.

Holmes nodded in agreement. "When you recovered, why did you not pursue the matter? You knew that you had not helped her in running away and believed her to be dead. Perhaps you thought that pressing any further would compromise Edward?"

Hewitt seemed to grasp this eagerly. "There was that to consider. I had already lost my mother, I couldn't bear to lose Ned as well. If Ned was afraid to put his trust in Bellows, I was not about to –" A sudden terror gripped our client as he realised what he was saying. He jumped in his chair and fell back heavily. "You have tricked me," he moaned. "I came to put my trust in you, and you trick me into saying more than ever I meant to. But you won't get any more out of me. That is all I have to say!"

Holmes waved a deprecatory hand. "I am not your Superintendent Bellows, Hewitt. You need not break your promise to your brother. If you would lead us to his room and explain –"

"No, it is not possible. Ned already fears I have betrayed the family by allowing you to come here. It will be all I can do tomorrow morning to assure him that he still may trust me. Does this mean you will not help me?"

"I cannot bring your mother back to life," said Holmes regretfully, "but I can show you her grave, and I believe that I will be able to name her murderer tomorrow."

This news brought Andrew Hewitt to his feet. It would have pitched him to the floor under buckling knees, but I caught him in time and steadied him.

"You know where she is buried?" cried the artist. "Tell me where, for the love of God!"

THE HUNT

Holmes refused to say more, despite Hewitt's entreaties, and I eventually piloted the artist back to his room.

After snatching a few hours' sleep, the next morning's early sun found Holmes and me upon the steep rise of land above Underhill Hall, where the hunt breakfast was to be held. From the crest we had an excellent view of all that might transpire below us, but we had stayed there no more than a few moments before Holmes gave a tug on my horse's rein and pointed down a mossy, rock-strewn slope which led to a more secluded spot just off the path by which we had come.

"There are advantages in having a painter as a client, Watson," observed my friend. "Hewitt described this spot to me in such perfect detail that I feel I have been here before. We may as well dismount and secure the horses while we wait. There may be riding enough later."

There had been riding enough already that morning. First we had allowed ourselves to be driven to East Quantock railway station, to give the impression that we would obediently board the early London train at Taunton, as ordered by Colonel Hewitt. Instead of doing so, however, we had hired a pair of horses in order to ride across country to where the riders were soon to gather for the meet. I had already forgotten the hurried breakfast we had taken at Coombehill hours ago, and I keenly felt the chill of those winds sweeping up to us from the open pastures below. Still, those very breezes were stripping away the clouds that had threatened to hover for yet another day, and I tried to take some cheer from the ever-brightening sky as I huddled against a tree with my coat collar high around my neck.

My friend's mood was not such as to make the vigil any less trying for the nerves. He sat now here, now there, now rubbing his hands, now shying pebbles down the hill. I took his nervous agitation as an ill omen, for normally at this stage in a case I should have expected to see this random energy suppressed by his supreme self-confidence and his intense powers of concentration. With a side-long glance he apprised my concern.

"Was there ever a plague so contagious as anxiety?" said he with a wry laugh. "I have contracted it from Hewitt, and now you are infected as well."

I grumbled that uncertainty was the greatest fuel of anxiety.

"Forgive me," Holmes apologised. "It slipped my mind that I had not spoken to you since I formed my plans. It is not the best scheme, but has the virtue of simplicity. Only heaven knows if there is a chance of success. Did you catch a glimpse of our friend the artist this morning? No? Well, you may take my word for it, he is a sorry sight. Between an excess of alcohol and a lack of sleep, he is the very picture of a troubled man. I cannot imagine that anyone who sees him can fail to speculate what is wrong with him. When he confides to brother Edward that the mystery of their mother's disappearance is about to be solved, I think he will be most convincing."

"How do you know he will confide in his brother?" I asked.

"Andrew begged me for permission to tell his brother that the mystery was about to be solved. When Andrew does not take his place in the hunt later today, I believe that Edward will alert the rest of the family. After breakfast Andrew Hewitt will join us here to exchange horses and clothing with me. I will follow along well behind the pack and see which of the hunting party finds himself with pressing business to attend to elsewhere. You will take Andrew safely back to his wife and her uncle, who have followed our example and declined to return to London. You will find them at the *Compton Arms* in the village."

"Can you expect to pass for Hewitt?" I queried. "You are both tall and dark, but he outweighs you by at least a stone."

"I intend to stay a good distance from the family members, I assure you," said Holmes. "It is a flawed plan, I grant you, but it is the best I can manage with the flawed data I have had to work with."

"But if you know where Elizabeth Hewitt is buried –" I expostulated.

"My dear fellow, I haven't the slightest idea where she is buried," said my friend. "We are in the position of huntsmen whose hounds have come to a check. We must cast around until we recover the line. However, in place of hounds, I have only words with which to draw my covert."

"You hope," I said slowly, "that the guilty man will reveal himself by attempting to move the body - or, maybe, attempt to bury another."

"Andrew Hewitt's," said Holmes crisply. "I want you to stay with him until I can rejoin you. Don't let him out of your sight, not even to be alone with his wife."

"And who will protect you while you impersonate Hewitt?"

Holmes patted his coat pocket. "I have another reliable friend besides you, Watson, though not nearly so companionable. Perhaps you would care to know my greatest fear concerning today's events?"

"And what is that?" I enquired, resigned to his foolhardiness.

"I fear that nothing at all may happen. Perhaps the colonel's wife merely deserted him after all. Perhaps she was actually murdered by those passing strangers of the old doctor's imagining. And yet, I cannot accept those explanations, not after hearing Hewitt's version of the story. I wish I knew what he was concealing and why, for it seems to have prevented him from taking any useful action in his mother's case. We have established that he is withholding information that he feels would be harmful to his brother, but what can that have to do with his mother's disappearance? I cannot believe he would keep silent if he believed that Edward Hewitt was their mother's killer."

"Is it so sure that the guilty party is one of the Hewitts?"

"No," replied Holmes, "but if it isn't the man I suspect, it will be a humiliating journey back to London for us."

"Can you tell me who it is that you suspect?" I asked.

"No, Watson. I guarantee that Hewitt will ask you the selfsame question the instant I have left the two of you alone. I don't like to think of the consequences if our client should believe he knows the solution to the case. His temperament is a bit too volatile for such knowledge, whether my theory should prove right or wrong."

"Did you believe all that Hewitt told you, then?"

"I believe that he is convinced of the truth of what he is saying. I am aware that you disapproved of my pressing him about the note. I know it upset him." Holmes spread his hands, "But his reaction struck me as being perfectly genuine. Either that or our artist should take to the boards when his wife retires from them. Further, his recollections rang true. Remember how well he could recall the events of the day, well before his shock. His memory worsens as the events of the night progress. That is consistent with both serious shock and a head injury, don't you agree?"

"I never doubted Hewitt's word for an instant," I said in reproach. "Now that you seem willing to take his word, you seem to think that his memory must be at fault. Where do you think he has made his mistakes?"

"I don't say he is wrong," said Holmes. "I say he did not see enough and I believe him when he claims he was too shaken to see more clearly. When first I met him, I thought he was a fool, but my opinion has changed. I should have known that anyone who could produce the kind of work that he does must have more to him than appearances would suggest. Now, Watson, here is a piece of specific information that will be of some practical use to you. I had the most informative conversation yesterday with Mr Vickers, the Master of Foxhounds. He tells me that today's hunt is in honour of Sir Gerald's birthday – hence the somewhat more elaborate breakfast in place of your everyday meet. It is the last major hunt of the season and the countryside will turn out to follow the hounds, making a perfect cover for one consulting detective. Mr Vickers tells me that, when the meet is at Underhill, he is expected to draw his first covert just north of the hill, provided the wind is favourable, as is the case today. Did you observe the place, Watson, just beyond the stream?"

"With woods upon the right?" I answered promptly.

"Correct," beamed Holmes. "My dear fellow, the out of doors is clearly your element. Very good. The hunt will proceed in that direction. You must wait here with your charge until you see that all the followers have crossed the stream; then it will be safe for you and Hewitt to go back down the hill towards the village. Ideally, you will meet no one along the way. If you do meet someone, use your best judgement, but trust no one."

Below we could hear the expected sequence of sounds: the arrival of the riders on horseback and in carriages, and the comparative silence when all went inside to have their hearty morning meal. I fancied that the scent of coffee wafted all the way to our hiding place. Then, at last, we heard the gathering of the hounds and the clattering of hooves of the horses as they made ready to start off upon the hunt. Our own mounts shifted nervously, as they sensed what was about to take place. On such short notice we had been forced to settle on a pair of horses whose hunting days were well behind them, but, even so, they seemed eager to participate.

A few minutes later we heard the approach of a single rider and Andrew Hewitt came into view on his magnificent roan. His face was as haggard as Holmes had reported, but his manner was remarkably cheerful. Swinging one long leg easily over the pommel of his saddle, he dropped lightly to the ground.

"Nobody saw me, Mr Holmes," he announced, "I'm sure of it. I did just as you said. I hid my gloves in my hat and then told Ned I had to go back for them. Since David and father aren't speaking to me, I had to deceive no-one else. I told Ned not to wait for me - that was right, wasn't it?"

Even Holmes smiled at the evident pleasure our client took in effecting his small deception. "Well done, Hewitt. Now, you understand that you must go with Watson and stay with him until I return."

Hewitt nodded and he and the detective exchanged coats. He frowned when he saw the revolver that Holmes was careful to transfer. "I only wish I understood the rest of it. Won't you even tell me what you expect will happen today? You don't intend to use that gun against any of my family, do you?"

"I don't intend to use it against anybody; it is for defence only," asserted Holmes. "Watson is also armed and will do his best to keep you safe in the event that I have misjudged the source of the danger."

"Danger?" queried Hewitt. "From whom? Mr Holmes, I have a right to know. Don't I, Watson? Don't I have the right to know?"

"Do as I tell you," said Holmes in a tone that brooked no nonsense, "and all will be well." Without waiting for a response he mounted Grenadier and spurred off down the rugged slope. Hewitt watched with me until horse and rider disappeared from view.

"What are the chances," murmured Hewitt casually, "of persuading you that we ought to follow him instead of retreating?"

I did not dignify the question with an answer, but simply looked hard at Hewitt.

He smiled and shrugged. "Ah, well, we would never stand a chance riding on these old bags of bones even if you were game for some sport. Mr Holmes must have selected these horses for their inability to thwart his plans. Look at this nag; I'll wager he is older than I am."

"Don't worry about the horses," I reproved. "They will carry us back to the village well enough."

"These stirrups are too short for me," complained Hewitt. "Oh, I see, this must be your horse, then. I'll take the horse Mr Holmes rode; he and I are near to the same height. Oh, it's maddening to stay here with no idea in the world what is going on. May we at least go to the top of the hill and watch the riders? They will all be looking ahead to the hounds; no one will notice us."

With some misgivings I agreed, but it was indeed a brave sight, the swirling pool of hounds floating out ahead of the company of long-legged horses. In the bright morning sunshine the sorrels were bright as new pennies, and the bays and chestnuts gleamed their own colours in contrast. Here and there a few greys, blacks and yellows added to the mottled brilliance that moved as one body of grace and strength. At the head rode the principal followers in their pink and I could pick out the colonel by his fine bay stallion and his military bearing. Behind were the other riders in their black and then came the rest of them on foot and in wagons and carriages of all descriptions, hoping for a sight of some sport, even if they could not themselves participate.

Following the moving ranks a single rider caught our attention. Holmes had circled round the hill so that he would appear to have come from the same direction as everyone else. His horse's easy canter brought him swiftly to within fifty yards or so of the pack, where he slowed to a restless walk. Beside me, Andrew Hewitt chuckled. "Grenadier won't like being last. See how Holmes holds him back. He goes well for him, though. I'd like to see them in full cry. But here we sit, hiding. Watson, I suspect Mr Holmes doesn't think very highly of me, does he?"

"I judge that his respect for you is increasing all the time," I replied. "He told me so just before you arrived. Does it matter?"

"I does to me," admitted my companion. "It is a very close contact with a man, to tell him the worst moments of your life. I've told you chaps things I have told only to Jane. I don't mind so much with you, Watson, because I know that you do your best to put yourself in another fellow's place, but Holmes considers me an idiot. I am in some ways, I suppose. Had I any brains of my own, I should have sorted out this mystery years ago. Now Holmes has done it in just a few days."

"Most of us seem slow when we compare ourselves with Sherlock Holmes," I commiserated. "Besides, you were injured and grief-stricken at the time. Holmes does not have those disadvantages."

With his eyes still fixed on the hunt below Andrew Hewitt casually asked, "Does Holmes truly believe I need a bodyguard?"

"He doesn't leave a client's safety to chance," I replied.

"You have a revolver? That looks as if it could do some damage. I've never fired a revolver, although I'm a fair hand with a bird gun. It's the eyes that make a crack shot, they say, and I have excellent eyes. Are you a good shot?"

I smiled modestly and admitted my prowess.

"But you wouldn't shoot me, would you?" said Hewitt, laughing. His demeanour suddenly changed and he stared at the scene below. "Good Lord, what are they doing down there?"

I turned sharply to look down at the colourful scene, but, so far as I could tell, Holmes was simply following the pack at a secure distance and I could discern nothing remarkable in what I saw below me. A scuffling sound from the hillside directly behind me was my first inkling that I had been played for a fool. By the time I could get to my feet, Hewitt was astride one of the horses and, before I had reached the other mount, he was halfway down the long slope. There was worse to come. When I put my toe into the stirrup iron, the whole saddle slid to the ground at my feet. Under the pretence of adjusting the stirrup leathers, Hewitt had contrived to undo the saddle girth instead. From below, I heard him cry out, "Sorry, cousin!"

My only chance to catch him was to follow without delay, so, with a bitter curse at my own lack of vigilance, I scrambled on to my horse's bare back and dug my heels into her flanks. There was a moment's hesitation as the beast turned her head towards me and rolled one large eye back, as if to question my choice to ride without the customary accoutrements. Another brisk kick and a shake of the reins convinced her that I was in earnest, and away we went, stumbling as fast as we could in pursuit while I clung for dear life to keep from preceding my mount down the incline.

Andrew Hewitt had reached level ground and was urging his horse as fast as it would go. In addition to the advantage he had of riding with a saddle, he had the better horse beneath him. He was also a superb horseman whose pace would have tested my abilities even had we been equally mounted. Given the rate that he was pulling ahead, it was only a question of minutes before he would elude me completely. I drew my revolver, thinking to lame his horse, but I feared for my aim on this uncertain ground and decided against pulling the trigger.

When Hewitt vanished into a wooded area on his right, I pulled up my lumbering steed and paused to think, no easy task with my brain whirling with the shame of having lost my charge within half an hour of his being entrusted to me. Even if no harm should actually come to Hewitt, I faced a dismal meeting with Holmes upon the conclusion of the case. Should the worst happen, I could not imagine how I could ever again expect my friend to put his confidence in me. Even more sobering was the thought of a meeting with Jane Hewitt. I suppose Holmes had been right when he said that I had almost begun to consider myself as her cousin. How could I bear it if I should have to bring her news that would break her heart?

Since I could not hope to pursue Hewitt to learn where he was going, I thought my best bet would be to return to the hilltop which would give me a view of so much of the countryside. It seemed most logical that his purpose was to join Holmes in following the hunt; perhaps I would be able to see him from the vantage point. Failing that, I might at least be able to overtake Holmes and give the alarm that his plan had fallen through. So to the crest of the hill I spurred my slow-gaited steed.

The hunt had proceeded to the covert beyond the stream, even as Holmes had predicted. I could see the hounds ranging wide among the rocks and stubble of gorse, while the riders ambled behind waiting for the real sport to begin. But look as I might, I could not discern the bright red horse with its tall slender rider. Where was Holmes?

Then I saw a movement in the corner of my eye. Far away from the hunt, moving in the opposite direction across open pasture, four horses were galloping at full tilt. One horse - the roan - ran ahead of the others. I did not need a closer look to realise that Holmes was being pursued by Colonel Hewitt and his two elder sons. In an instant, I was heading down the path as fast as my old horse could carry her ill-equipped rider. This immediate danger to Holmes superseded my search for Hewitt. If the rest of the Hewitts were the villains in the case, Andrew Hewitt would be safe enough following the hunt, while Holmes and I dealt with his enemies miles away.

It was no easier tracking these four than it had been to follow the elusive artist. I had not gone very far before I began to appreciate the significance of the saddle as an invention for the comfort of mankind, but, in truth, I was less daunted by the perils of bareback riding than I was by the clear impossibility of my ever overtaking the riders ahead. I picked up their traces with little difficulty on the damp and open ground, but I had lost all sight and sound of them, and I feared that any help I might offer Holmes would come too late. But I pressed on, in large part because I could think of nothing more useful to do.

I must have travelled a mile or more when the track I was following suddenly veered off to a broad pathway into a thick wood. I had to go more slowly, keeping my head well down to avoid the treacherous overhanging branches. Then, without warning, I burst into a clearing full upon my quarry. All were dismounted and standing in a sinister tableau before me, Holmes at the centre with David and Edward Hewitt upon either side of him, holding his arms tightly to prevent his escape. The old colonel faced the three with his riding crop poised threateningly, but I felt a wave of relief pass over me just the same, that Holmes was alive and apparently unhurt as yet.

After listening to the pounding of my horse's hooves, the sudden silence was eerie and menacing when I pulled to a halt. As I reined up in full view of them, Holmes favoured me with an angry glance, which I knew referred to my failure to take Andrew Hewitt back to the village. It was entirely characteristic of this remarkable man that, faced with imminent danger though he was, he displayed no emotion save that of annoyance that his instructions had not been explicitly carried out. In any event, I was not inclined to leave him in peril for long; another moment saw my revolver trained upon his attackers. I would have preferred to dismount and take a better aim, but I feared that my legs would be too unsteady after my unaccustomed ride.

"Let him go," I ordered. "I don't want to shoot, but I will if I must."

"Watson," said Sherlock Holmes mildly, "this won't do. Put away that gun. Better yet, let Colonel Hewitt hold it for you."

I stared open-mouthed at Holmes for a moment. I was not used to question his judgment, but these instructions were completely incomprehensible to me.

"Give Colonel Hewitt the gun," he repeated urgently, "and tell us quickly what has happened to Andrew."

I dismounted and placed my revolver into the old soldier's hand.

"There you have your demonstration of our good faith, Colonel," said Holmes.

Laurence Hewitt nodded to his sons, who obediently released their prisoner. All eyes now turned to me, and I quickly explained what had taken place after Holmes had left me to guard Andrew.

Ned Hewitt stepped forward eagerly when he heard my story. "I taught Andrew that trick of undoing the girth, Papa. I must have played it on him a dozen times when we were lads. Dr Watson is telling us the truth, I'm sure of it."

"Then where has he gone, Mr Holmes?" asked the father.

"Your son has solved the mystery of his mother's death on his own, and has gone to deal out justice himself. He is bound for Dr Farthingale's cottage."

Ned Hewitt struck his palm to his forehead in dismay. "Andrew has made fools of us all! Oh, Mr Holmes, I see it now. He led you to believe that he would follow your advice, but instead he instructed me how best to waylay you. He has played us all against one another so that he could be the one to avenge Mother's death."

"Exactly!" cried Holmes. "He has started before us, but his horse is slow. If we ride like the devil to the village, we may be able to prevent a further tragedy."

Colonel Hewitt stared hard at them both. "And you say it is Farthingale he is after?"

"There is no doubt of it," responded Holmes. "Let us ride to the doctor's cottage without delay."

I could see the Colonel come to a decision. "Very well. But I hold you responsible for my son's fate. May God help you if he has come to any harm. Watson, mount the black, if you please. We cannot wait for you and your plough horse, and I would rather not let you out of my sight."

David Hewitt's mouth dropped. "You are giving him my horse! What am I to ride?"

"That should be obvious, Davey," answered his father with a wave towards the tired old mare who had brought me thus far. "You may join us at Farthingale's when you are able. Come, gentlemen!"

Holmes boosted me on to the back of David Hewitt's tall black hunter, and I was instantly aware of the seething energy beneath me, so different from the aging mare whom I had badgered and cajoled for every ounce of her speed. I had never before sat astride so fine and fiery an animal, and I could only pray that I would manage to stay seated and be of some service to Holmes and to Andrew Hewitt when we reached the village.

Never have I ridden so hard and so fast as we rode that day. We shot through the woods, as if we supposed the branches would part for us, emerging into the brilliant sunshine so abruptly that I was momentarily blinded. The roads were not a direct enough route for an anxious father, so we travelled overland, an easy matter at first over the open pasture. Then we veered down a slope towards a low stone wall. There was no chance for me to circle around it and still remain with the others; I had to clear it.

Four lengths ahead of me, Edward Hewitt stiffened his legs, set himself well back in the saddle and gathered his horse under him for the leap. His father was just behind him, and both soared over the wall with room to spare. In the next instant, Sherlock Holmes made his approach. He adopted a peculiar position just before the jump, bending low and forward over the horse's neck, until I feared that he would surely fall at the landing. He had no such difficulty after all, and then it was my turn. I had a sense that this first barrier was the crucial test for me. If all went well here, it would mean that I had not lost the ability to take a horse over a jump. If I failed - it made my face burn to imagine how far Holmes' respect for me would fall were I to slip from my saddle or drop too far behind. My only chance of redeeming myself for my failure to guard Andrew Hewitt was to make no more mistakes that day. I tried not to think any more of the possibility that my failure might be the cause of our client's death.

I prepared myself as the Hewitts had, and my horse took to the air. His strength and skill more than made up for my deficiencies as a rider, and we struck the ground cleanly on the other side with no more ill effects than a racing heart - my own, of course. My gallant hunter clearly thought nothing of so trivial a barrier, and I realised that if I could simply stay with him and not impede him in any way, he would manage for both of us. Best of all, this initial success revived memories of the hard riding I had done in my younger days, and gave me confidence. I soon forgot my fears and let the importance of our purpose - and, yes, the thrill of the hunt - overtop my concern for my own safety.

Our breakneck pace was devouring the distance between us and our destination. I tried to judge how far ahead of us Andrew Hewitt might be, balancing his head start against the inferiority of his mount, and I arrived at the conclusion that there was every chance of our being in time - provided that we were going in the right direction! David Hewitt's separation from the group worried me; although the Colonel had given me his son's horse ostensibly so that he should be able to keep an eye on me, it occurred to me that it was a clever way to give David the opportunity to make mischief elsewhere. I had never known Holmes to be mistaken once he had made his mind up about a case, but anything was possible in this rushing confusion.

The other three seemed to have no doubts. Expert riders all, they surged ahead of my pace by a dozen lengths or more. It was thrilling to watch them: the roan and the two dark bays with their pink-coated riders swaying above their flowing backs. Holmes gave a backward look from time to time, but these glances seemed more to assure himself that I was keeping up with the group. At one stage we had to take a five-foot hedgerow, and I had something of a struggle regaining my proper seat after the jolt of landing on the further side. When I was on an even keel once more, I happened to look to Holmes; I caught him watching me again, but this time he was suppressing a grin.

At last we emerged on to the road into the village. It was as well that virtually all the district was out to view the hunt, for we surely would have trampled anyone unfortunate enough to be in our path that day. This was the sort of riding at which I used to excel - flat and fast - and, as I was smaller and lighter than the others, including Holmes in those days, my eager horse now had nothing in the way of his closing the gap between us and the horses ahead. I was riding alongside my friend when first we sighted the pair of stone columns that marked the pathway to the cottage where Dr Hugh Farthingale lived and worked.

As we approached, we all saw Andrew Hewitt's sweat-darkened horse, untethered and cropping at the sparse early spring lawn where his rider had abandoned him in his haste to enter the dwelling. Holmes had been correct so far - but were we in time? The absolute stillness all around boded ill for that hope. The four of us flung ourselves from our horses and dashed - or, in my case, hobbled - to the front door, Holmes in the lead. He did not pause to knock, but pushed straight inside, as if he knew precisely where to go.

    I was directly behind Colonel Hewitt when he got his first glimpse past Holmes into the sun-streaked sitting room, and I never wish to hear again so anguished a sound as the moan he made when he saw his youngest son stretched before us on the floor. No wound was visible, but Andrew Hewitt was utterly motionless, and his jacket and cravat were askew as if he had been subdued in a violent struggle. Oddly, there was a pillow beneath his supine head, as if his attacker had wanted him to rest more easily. The old soldier growled a vicious oath and threw himself to his knees at the side of his son.

THE CONFESSION

I followed close behind, ready to offer my services if there were still the least chance of a doctor's skills being put to use. As I leant down towards the fallen man, my senses smarted from a pungent odour. "Chloroform!" I cried. "He is breathing." I looked around me for help. "Bring me a basin and a pitcher of water," I called. Ned Hewitt and Sherlock Holmes swiftly disappeared in search of the items. "His pulse is strong," I assured the father. "He'll suffer no ill effects when he wakes, save a burning sensation where the chemical was applied."

Colonel Hewitt's hard eyes glistened with joyful tears and he bit nervously at his trembling lip, as he reached out to confirm with his own touch that the son he thought he had lost was truly alive. The basin soon was brought and the father insisted on bathing his son's face himself, brushing the wet cloth tenderly over the irritated skin, as he called his name repeatedly. He glanced away from his charge for a moment and whispered to me, "Even an old fool like me will learn a lesson the third time it is repeated. When he wakes this time, he'll find his father changed. Damn you, Andrew, open your eyes!"

At my suggestion we moved the unconscious man to the greater comfort of the couch to await the moment when he would obey his hovering father's command to wake. While I waited, apart from the family, it occurred to me that Holmes had not yet rejoined us. Only then did I remember that there was still a case to solve and a criminal to bring to justice, beyond the poignant family reconciliation that had occupied my attention. Holmes, of course, had not forgotten for an instant. Leaving the Hewitts to tend their own, I went in search of my friend.

I took a quick look at the living quarters adjoining the sitting room and, not seeing him there, went down the hall towards the business wing of the house. I finally found him in the doctor's surgery, but he was not alone. Before him upon the consulting room couch, his face the colour of cold ashes, Dr Farthingale lay as still as could be.

As I took in the scene, Holmes turned his head towards me and nodded towards a syringe and a small vial on the nearby table. "Suicide. Morphine, I believe. How is your patient?"

I reassured my friend on the latter score, but asked, "What has happened here?"

"The explanation is inside," he replied, holding up a large manilla envelope addressed in bold black letters. "This is for Mister Andrew Hewitt. Perhaps we should deliver it to him."

By the time we returned to the sitting room, the young painter was awake and looking around him in a rather dazed fashion. He seemed to know where he was, however, for he smiled apologetically at the sight of the detective. "I've spoilt your plans, haven't I, Mr Holmes?"

"You have," answered my friend in a far gentler tone than I would have expected him to use under the circumstances.

"Has Doctor Hugh escaped?" There was no mistaking the hopeful note in Andrew Hewitt's voice.

"Dr Farthingale has taken his own life," Holmes replied. "That is an escape of a sort. He gave you chloroform so that you could not prevent his suicide."

Hewitt touched his nose and lips gingerly. "Poor chap. He crept up behind me after I came in the front door. I tried to shake him off, but the stuff blinded me and then I became so drowsy that I could not struggle any more. Now we shall never know the truth."

Holmes handed our client the envelope, which was labelled, 'For Andrew Fitzhenry, upon my death'.

Edward Hewitt snatched the envelope away from his brother. "Don't ever open it, Andrew."

"Ned, what are you doing?" cried Andrew. The barrister had lunged towards the mantle as if to pitch the document into the fire, but his intent was frustrated, as there was no sign of a spark within the grate. A moment later, Sherlock Holmes had retrieved the envelope and placed it in the hands of the youngest son once more.

Andrew Hewitt looked from the envelope to his father and brother. It was obvious that he longed to open the missive that would explain the mystery of his mother's death, but his loyalty to his brother was a powerful deterrent.

Holmes broke the stalemate by announcing, "I can spare you any further exertions, gentlemen, by telling you that I already had some inkling that your father was responsible for the death of Collins, the groom."

"That is a lie!" shouted the elder son.

I looked at his father, who seemed not to have taken notice of the slight scuffle waged by the fireplace or of anything that had been said. His arm encircled Andrew's shoulders and the old man seemed unwilling to look anywhere but his son's face. Holmes went on speaking to Edward Hewitt.

"What other conclusion could an intelligent man reach, once he was in possession of the facts? When Andrew told me that Collins was alive when he left him and dead when he returned, when I knew that Colonel Hewitt was paying blackmail to Dr Farthingale and an income to Collins' widow and children, and when I learned that you, Edward, had gone well out of your way to keep your father from learning that a negligent servant had caused your brother's recent accident - I had to conclude that there was some guilt attached to your father in regard to Collins' death. It also followed that you knew the truth of it."

"You can conclude what you like," snapped Edward Hewitt. "The truth is, I killed Collins, and my brother knows it. Don't you, Andrew? Look at my brother's face if you suppose that I am inventing this story. He did not see me do it, but he has always known that I did. My father is innocent."

"Your father," interposed Colonel Hewitt, stirring himself, "is prepared at last to tell the truth. The time has come. You have kept my secret long enough, dear Ned." The Colonel rose from the couch where his son lay and drew himself up. "Mr Holmes, is it true that the contents of that envelope will prove that Farthingale killed my wife and that my boy, Andrew, knew nothing of it?"

"I believe so," nodded Holmes.

"Then open it without a moment's delay. I never meant to kill the groom, but he died at my hands all the same, and, if the time has come for me to take my punishment for it, so be it. Open it, Andrew, my boy. Read for all to hear."

"Yes, Papa." Andrew Hewitt withdrew the envelope's contents, which were several sheets of notepaper folded together and one hastily torn scrap that had been creased separately from the rest. He took the scrap first and read aloud:

"'My dear Andrew - I hope you will forgive my cowardice today. I could not face you with the truth and, when I saw this morning that you had guessed my guilt, I determined never to live to see you curse me for what I have done. Today I shall kill your mother's killer, and justice will be served at last. Perhaps when you read my story you may find it possible to forgive me. May you live long and happily with the beautiful lady you have married. Your loving friend, Hugh.' Ned, would you mind very much reading the rest for me?" asked the artist softly. "My eyes are still stinging."

"Give it to me," said his brother, taking the remainder of the sheets from Andrew's hands. "'My dear Andrew, I write this in anticipation of the day when my wretched life will be over and I shall go to the punishment that I know awaits me for my sins. Beware, my dear lad, of outliving your immortal soul, as I have done. In my old age, when I should have been contented and wise, I chose to make one last selfish lunge at passion, and it has caused nothing but misery for me and those I loved the most: you and your lovely mother.

"'Ever since your mother first came to Somerset as a young woman, I loved her for her beauty of face and soul, but this love remained within the bounds of a deep friendship. It was not until some years after my own wife's death that I realised my lonely heart had taken me beyond that boundary into a place from which no effort of will could return me. I found that I loved your mother as madly as any young boy in his first passion of love.

"'I never told anyone this, of course. Thank God, you never saw my foolish note to her in which I declared my love, and that you never recognised how deep my feelings ran. You have a right to see her reply to that note. I enclose it here for you, to dispel any doubts you may have had about her angel's soul. Show it to your father if you so wish. I have wronged him as much as I have wronged you, and this may mean something to him.'"

"Here it is," said Edward Hewitt. "'Dr Farthingale - I find myself both touched and honoured by the sentiments you expressed to me. However, you must appreciate that

I cannot in any way return them, or even so much as allow myself to hear them again. I am a married woman in religion and law and, most of all, in heart and mind as well. If I ever misled you into believing otherwise, I beg your forgiveness. I looked upon you as a friend - no, as a brother - but I see now that this was unwise and unfair to you. From now on, we must seek to avoid those situations which might lead to temptation for you and sorrow for all of us. As much as I value your precious friendship, I cannot let anything jeopardise my happiness with my honoured husband and my three splendid sons. Please never speak to me of love again, or I must put an end to all communication between us. E.F.H.'"

Andrew took the note from his brother and offered it silently to his father, who folded it away into his pocket without a word. Edward Hewitt again took up the body of the doctor's letter and continued reading aloud.

"'This exchange of correspondence took place two weeks before your mother's death, during which time she took care to avoid me. I was frantic with love and frustration. I became obsessed with the notion that I only needed to plead my case in person to sway her to love me as I loved her. I wrote her another message, begging for an interview. She refused. I could hardly bear it. I decided I would have to trick her into seeing me.

"'Norah Dudley's illness gave me the opportunity I sought. Never was a doctor so attentive to a patient as I to Mrs Dudley, knowing as I did that Bess Hewitt would not fail to visit her ailing friend. In fact, I learned the day before her visit that she was due to come next afternoon.

"'Your father was suspicious of me, however, and I knew I must ensure that he would not follow his wife. Therefore I wrote a note establishing a false rendezvous with your mother and made certain that it was left where your father could not fail to find it. Knowing that such a man of action would surely follow where my note led, I guaranteed myself a clear field to plead my case with his wife. I hoped to convince her to leave him and come away with me to a new life. I swear on my soul that I never meant her any harm. Yet, how could I hope to gain a sinful end without sinful means and woeful consequences?

"'That evening I visited the Dudleys, knowing full well that Bess would be there. My plan was to stay until she was nearly ready to depart. I had contrived to put a bottle of drugged wine into the hands of that besotted driver of hers, and I hoped that when he was judged unfit to take her home, she would be forced to accept my offer of a ride. Instead, everything went wrong. She suspected my motives from the first and lingered for some time at the Dudleys. I had to leave before her lest I create suspicion in the minds of others. When I looked in on Collins as I left, he appeared not to have touched the wine I gave him. On every count my plans were failing. Nevertheless, I hoped still for a word or two with her, and so, instead of returning directly to the village, I drove along the Bridgwater Road in the direction of Coómbehill, and waited for her at the crossroads just before the stone bridge.

"'Barely half an hour later, her cart appeared on the wooded lane. My heart leapt when I saw that she was the driver and that Collins was in a heap behind her. He had drunk the wine at last! My plan seemed to be working after all! I called out to her, but, instead of stopping for me, she whipped up her horse and pulled away. Fool that I was, murderer that I am, I pursued her, heedless of the consequences. She was unable to handle the horse and cart and the chase ended just after the bridge, as you saw. When the cart left the road and overturned, she was thrown against the bole of a tree. She was alive when I reached her, but it was obvious that her injuries were severe. I scarcely paused to examine Collins, who was lying under the cart without a mark on him, though he was unconscious and his breathing was unsteady. I left him there and gathered up Bess Hewitt. My one thought was that I might save her if I could get her to my surgery.

"'But it was not to be. She breathed her last on the way to my cottage, having never opened her eyes again. Still, I laboured for an hour or more, praying for some miracle to undo the consequences of my folly. When I realised it was no use, I lost my bearings for a time. I stumbled around the house, trying to perform routine tasks as if nothing were amiss. I stabled my horse properly. I changed from my soiled clothing into my nightshirt. I took a whiskey to try to sleep, but it had no effect whatsoever.

"'Then came your knock on my door. When I heard your voice calling my name, I thought my heart would break, to think that I should have to tell you what I had done. I swear to you that I went to the door with no intention of concealing the truth of what had happened. But when I saw your handsome young face before me, so like your dear mother's, my tongue froze to the roof of my mouth. You must have thought me drowsy from the late hour as you helped me hitch my horse, but the truth is that I was in a state of utter shock. I heard you tell me all about Collins. That was when I told you my first lie - that your mother had planned to stay at Primrose Hill that night. It was so much easier to lie than to face the truth.

"'I might yet have found my courage had your father not been at the bridge when we arrived. He knew your mother had not remained with the Dudleys, and knew from them that I had seen her. He seemed half mad and I knew he suspected me. I could see that Collins was dead, lying some yards from where I had left him. It entered my mind that your father might have killed him, and I was fearful that the same fate might happen to me should I reveal the truth to him out there in that dark and lonely place. There was no telling how even you or your brother might react to the knowledge that I was directly responsible for your mother's death. And so I told more lies, for fear of my wretched life. And as I lied, it seemed that the lie made a good deal more sense than the truth. I had last seen Bess Hewitt at the Dudleys at seven o'clock, I thought. I had gone home and nodded over a book, and perhaps dreamt the whole horrible episode. How I wished it might be so. I willed it to be so!

"'My lies were good enough to get me away from Colonel Hewitt and that awful place. I took Collins' body back to Coombehill. I broke the news to his widow, poor pretty thing with two babes. Then I began to think more clearly, now that I was not so frightened. I examined Collins carefully while I waited for you all to return. His neck was indeed broken, but, when I looked closely at the injury, it was clear that the break must have been caused by his fall from the cart. No human hands could have damaged the vertebrae in such a way. If the Hewitts were at fault, it must have been that they had moved the man carelessly, severing the spinal cord between the pressure of the damaged bones. Here I saw some hope for my own case. If Laurence or Ned Hewitt had killed Collins by mere accident, it might be easier for them to understand how it was that I had done the same to Bess. I gathered my courage once more.

"'However, when I saw you unconscious and with your head all bloody, I lost my nerve forever. I knew immediately that your father had done it, no matter what story they had about a fall from your horse. If he could split open the head of his own son, God only knew what he would do to me if he learnt the truth. At the same time, I made up my mind that he should suffer. I taxed him with the murder of Collins, telling him that I could see he had broken the man's neck, even as he had manhandled his own son. To my satisfaction, he protested that Collins regained his senses briefly, and that he - your father, that is - had only just given him a shaking out of desperation to hear what had become of his wife. The man had fallen dead in an instant, he said. I told him I would say nothing to the constable, but I insisted on taking charge of you. From that day, the Hewitts could not deny me anything I asked. Oh, I never wanted the money. I had you, my dear boy. I kept you from your father's house and turned your heart against him as best I could. You loved me better in those days than you loved your own father.

"'For a time, your father still seemed suspicious that I might try to leave East Quantock and join your mother somewhere, but, as the weeks and months went by, even so stubborn a man as he could see that he was mistaken. It never occurred to him that I had caused her death; I had difficulty in believing that myself. The marvel of it was that the police never suspected me. While they searched the roads and ditches, I buried your mother and all traces of my guilt. The note I had written merely to ensure your father's absence was somehow judged to be proof positive that your mother had decamped with someone else. I could understand how that imbecile Bellows might have jumped to such an outrageous conclusion, but I could only wonder what lay in your father's heart that he was able to accept so easily the notion that his wife should have left him. I had always supposed he was unworthy of her, and nothing proved it so surely as his lack of faith in her virtue.

"'Your presence in my house was such a joy to me, but it was a worry too. You alone knew in your heart that she was dead. Your two souls had always been linked with the tenderest bonds of mother and son - how could you fail to know that her soul had left this world? How often I worried as we sat together before my fire and you confided that you felt her spirit with you. I feared she might well lead you to her burial place. Then too, the sight of your face became a reproach to me, recalling the dear face that I should never see again. And so I told you to leave this place and seek a home far from your memories. Can you deny that it was the best advice I could have given you?

"'I know that I have not long to live. My lungs are all inflamed and they are pressing my shrivelled heart to death. I have for some months contemplated taking the shorter road to the eternal punishment, but whichever route I take, do not grieve for me. Forgive me if you can, my beloved boy, and, if you can, pray also that God may forgive me. The pain I caused you I never meant to cause, and I hope that, by telling you the truth now, I can set your heart at ease a little. Forgive your father too, my boy. You know that is what your mother would have wished you to do.

"'You will find her remains in the northeast corner of the basement. I put some shelves there to conceal the spot from my housekeeper. Please believe that I buried her with all respect and spoke many a prayer for her as I did.

"'If it is possible, please have me buried next to my wife. Had I remained faithful to her memory, I might be with her in paradise now. Hugh Farthingale.'"

Outside the open window a group of sparrows were chirping in the trees, exulting in the glories of the spring sunshine, but within the room we were a much more sombre group. By some tacit regard for rank, we all seemed to be waiting for Colonel Hewitt to say something, but he was a long time composing himself. At last he made an effort to speak, but the sound was choked and unintelligible. Clearing his throat he tried again and now his voice was thick, but serviceable.

"I was blind. I could not see for anger, or I would not see for fear of answering for Collins' death. I thought I'd killed him: he came partially to his senses just as I arrived. Ned tried to question him, but he would only speak of a bottle. Now I see that he was trying to tell us that he knew the wine had been drugged, but that night, I simply thought he wanted another drink. I took him by the shoulders to shake some sense into his sodden skull; the next I knew, he was dead at my feet. Farthingale was right, you know. I was half mad that night. After waiting all those hours at the *Red Lion* with that cursed note in my pocket, only to learn that I had been made a fool of by its author, I was all too ready to believe that I had actually murdered a man with my bare hands."

The colonel steadied his grip on his youngest son, as if the tears that clouded his eyes had forced him to rely on his sense of touch to assure him that Andrew was still there. He drew a shuddering breath and went on. "All I could think of when I saw you was your Paris pranks, and how your mother had lied to me for your sake at that time. You and she had so many secrets from me. I knew she was not always happy, that I should have given her a greater portion of my time than I thought I could spare from the running of the estate. I was convinced that you must know of her whereabouts. When you accused me of killing her, it was too much. How close I came to losing you both that night! Now I see that I am to blame for letting the man who caused your mother's death go unpunished for so long. If I had had the courage to admit my own guilt! If I had listened to you! But I fear we have been at war for so long now that not even the best intentions can bring us peace. It is too late."

"No!" pleaded his son. "Why should it be too late? We were both cruelly deceived and we –"

He broke off at a sound outside that took Sherlock Holmes to the window.

"It is Mr David Hewitt at last," announced Holmes, "and he has brought a guest."

David Hewitt burst into the house, followed by another man, who looked about him uncertainly before he spoke.

"What seems to be the trouble, Colonel Hewitt?"

Edward Hewitt and his father exchanged a glance, then the barrister stepped forward to meet the local Superintendent. "I have a document here which it may interest you to read. When you have done so, we are all willing to answer whatever questions you may have to ask us."

THE EXPLANATION

By the time we had recounted the entire story to the stolid arm of the local law, not one of us had the energy or the will to do anything more than wend our way back to Coombehill for a light supper and, finally, the comfort of our beds. Andrew Hewitt was too unsteady to sit a horse and so I drove him home in Dr Farthingale's gig, only too glad for my own aching muscles to avoid riding horseback again that day. It did my heart good to see how tenderly Colonel Hewitt helped his son to the carriage seat, and how he rode beside us every step of the way as if he were keeping guard over a precious cargo. And it was satisfying to see the loving scene at Coombehill, as the father relinquished his son into the care of the young bride. After a long day of suspense and worry, she was nearly frantic with relief at the sight of her somewhat bedraggled spouse, and she could not help but hover and flutter about him as we helped him to his room. This was the first time during her stay that her new family had seen her without a veneer of poise and self-control, but under the circumstances I think her tears only served to endear her to them all in a way that her customary self-possession never could have done.

I cannot speak for the others, but when at last I found my pillow, I did not wake to the light of day until the middle of the next afternoon. My head felt clear and my heart was light, but every inch of my body throbbed and ached from the pounding I had taken the previous day. I felt fortunate to be able to manage the effort of ringing the bell for tea; the prospect of dressing and going downstairs - stairs! - for a meal was out of the question.

With my tea came two visitors: Andrew Hewitt and Sherlock Holmes. Hewitt looked quite well, with only a trace of redness around his mouth and nose to show for his experience. "We were beginning to have concern for you, cousin," said he cheerfully. "I never knew a man sleep so long at one go."

"I was very tired," I admitted, "and a little sore." I caught Holmes' eye. "I am extremely sore."

"A hot bath in mustard will do wonders for that,"

advised the artist, and moved to help me with my pillows, which in my stiffness were proving recalcitrant. "I feel simply awful that you are hurt," continued Hewitt. "You have a perfect right to be furious with me. Let me butter your toast for you. Are you angry?"

How could one be angry in the face of his open and heartfelt contrition and his charming ways? "No, I am not. But I would prefer to butter my own toast, if you don't mind. Won't you both sit down? You'll give me a crick in my neck from looking up at you. You look rather better today than you did yesterday, Hewitt."

Andrew Hewitt smiled ruefully. "I am coming to grips with it all. I feel so sorry for Doctor Hugh. How could anyone fail to forgive him, poor soul! To have all his hopes end as they did, when he only wanted to declare his love for her. Now that I know the truth, I can't imagine how it was that I never guessed how he truly felt about my mother. It's small wonder he couldn't bring himself to admit that he had killed her. Perhaps he might have confessed that very night had I not provoked my father into splitting my head open as I did. I was so proud of my closeness to my mother, who would always take my part against Father, even when I was in the wrong. Without realising it, I may have encouraged Dr Farthingale to believe that Mother and Father could be drawn apart."

At his elbow, Sherlock Holmes stirred. "There is no need to chastise yourself, Mr Hewitt. We are all responsible for our own actions and Farthingale was no exception. He exploited your family's differences for his own ends, first in his attempt to win your mother and later in his scheme to hide his guilt."

"He has suffered for it, poor man," said Hewitt, "and he made some amends by clearing the mystery up for us. I am thankful that my mother's death was more an accident than an act of malice, and that she did not suffer. Father has been magnificent, don't you think? Did you ever see such composure? I couldn't say two words to Superintendent Bellows without my handkerchief in front of my eyes, but Father told the whole story without a tremor. What will happen to him, Mr Holmes? And to Ned? Will they be arrested?"

"It is possible that there could be some criminal proceedings," Holmes said slowly, "though not in the death of Collins; the evidence of Dr Farthingale's confession removes all blame from your family. In the matter of obstructing the course of justice, however, you are all guilty. Even you, Mr Hewitt. In the eyes of the law, you ought to have spoken up when your brother told you he had killed Collins."

"He told me it had been an accident," averred Hewitt. "There was no question in my mind that Ned hadn't the least thing to do with whatever had happened to Mother, and I couldn't see the point in his being sent off to prison, when I had already lost someone very dear to me."

Holmes rose and went to the window as if he did not want to look Andrew Hewitt in the face. "It was clever of your brother to shoulder the blame, knowing that you would be more willing to protect him than your father."

"Yes, he was quite right about that," admitted Hewitt. "I was so angry with father in those days, there is no telling what I might have said or done, but I would have gone to my grave with a secret for Ned."

Holmes took out his cigarette case and offered it to each of us. As we began to smoke, he smiled mysteriously at our client. "It would have been better in the long run if your brother had told the police what he told you. You both overestimated the emphasis they would have placed upon your brother's connection with Sally Collins."

Hewitt stared at my friend and then laughed one of his nervous laughs. "I am past being amazed at what you discover, Mr Holmes."

"This is anything but amazing," retorted Holmes. "When you told me the history of Mrs Collins' fortunes, it occurred to me that it might be more than a coincidence which brought her to Somerset when her husband was in desperate need of a situation. I took you at your word when you denied any romantic entanglement with her and I was able to eliminate your father and your brother David, who never go to London, according to reliable local sources. This left brother Edward, who might easily have been in London reading for the law some years ago. When I recalled your look of astonishment and fear at my enquiry concerning your brother's broken engagement, I realised I had struck an unexpected vein.

I had merely meant to ask about the cause of David's grudge against you, but you imagined I had somehow learnt more than you wished me to know about Mrs Collins and brother Edward. He had only just informed you that Watson and I had gone to see her at home, which also explained your eagerness to tell us your dreadful tale about Miss Helena."

"If you knew all this, Mr Holmes," said Hewitt, "it was awfully decent of you not to say anything to Bellows yesterday. You see, my brother still has hopes that somehow he and Sally might be able to marry after all. He certainly deserves happiness; you cannot imagine how noble he has been."

"Was he paying blackmail to Collins all these years?" queried Holmes.

"Collins tried something of the sort, but my brother would not allow it," Hewitt claimed. "After all, what had he to be ashamed of? His past connection with Sally was perfectly honourable. They met in London while he was studying law. As I told you, her father owned a business and there was no reason why they should not marry, except that she was so young and Ned not yet established in his career. However, when he spoke of waiting a few years for the wedding, she became angry and foolishly turned to the next man who showed any interest in her - Collins, as ill chance would have it. He was eager for marriage to his employer's daughter, of course. Then her father died, leaving the business to a cousin, rather than allow Collins to get his hands on it through Sally. The rest I've told you. When they came here and Collins threatened to reveal Sally's identity, my brother challenged him to do so, and that ended all talk of blackmail.

"Nevertheless, Ned would not let Sally suffer because of who she had married, and he and I made sure that Mother would intercede in favour of Collins, so that he would always have a place here, though it tormented my poor brother so to see the woman he still loved in the power of that miserable man. She still loved him too, and was foolish enough to let her husband see it. I couldn't have blamed Ned had he killed the man intentionally, though, of course, such an action was beyond him. At any rate, the manner of Collins' death, rather than freeing

Sally for marriage with my brother, made matters rather worse. There would be talk enough that a Hewitt had married a former servant, but Ned lived in fear that any action on his part would arouse suspicion over Collins' death, and risk putting the law on to Father. Good Lord, now that we are well out of it, what a dreadful tangled mess it seems to have been! We were all so afraid of the truth. Each thought he was acting for the best, but the truth would have been the best by far. Who knows what might happen now? I have a wonderful sense that we have all been given a chance to start again. Assuming that there are no criminal charges, there is nothing to prevent Ned from marrying the woman he loves at last."

"And what of your other brother?" I asked.

"David truly believed that Mother had deserted us," answered Hewitt. "Coming after his experience with Helena, it was too much. Now that he knows Mother was true to Father after all, it has taken away much of his bitterness. He spoke to my wife today, can you imagine that? It was only a brief 'Good morning', but it was a very civil greeting. Who knows, by this time next week, he may have worked his way to becoming almost pleasant. Do you want anything else, Watson? I'll ring for you, if you like. Here, let me take those tea things out of your way."

"Hewitt!" I protested with a laugh. "There is no need for you to mollycoddle me so."

"But there is," he contradicted. "You don't know what I've had to listen to from Mr Holmes about how beastly I was to play that trick upon you. I accept it was a shabby way to treat a fellow who was ready to risk his life for me, but I had to do what I did. You understand, don't you, cousin? Whatever he might have done, Dr Hugh was my friend, and I wanted to see him alone so that I could hear his version of the story before I told anyone else what I knew. I was afraid that you and Mr Holmes would not understand that. I knew my father would not."

"It was a foolish and dangerous thing to do," said Holmes, shaking his head. "Men have been killed when they have let it be known that they have guessed another's guilt. If you had told us the entire truth, it would have spared everyone a great deal of trouble. We would have been your allies. After all, Farthingale was in the forefront of my mind as a possible suspect."

"You might have told me that," Hewitt said. "I thought you suspected my father and my brother David."

"So I did," said Holmes blandly. "And brother Edward as well."

Hewitt gasped.

"He made such a point of being in your presence for much of that fatal evening," explained Holmes, "that I had to consider the possibility that he was trying to give himself an alibi. But my curiosity is piqued to hear how you solved the case, Hewitt. What did you recall after three and a half years that finally led you to the truth?"

"Very well," said Hewitt, seemingly slightly embarrassed. "After I'd told you my story, when Watson took me back to Jane's room, I thought I should never be able to sleep a wink for mulling over your claim that you knew where Mother was buried. Jane and I talked and talked, and I fell asleep with that thought in my mind: where was Mother's grave? Near dawn I had a dream. I was lying in the bed where I used to sleep in Dr Farthingale's cottage and I could hear the snow tapping on the window outside. I got up to look out and I saw the scene as I painted it - you know the painting?"

We both nodded.

"I suddenly saw there was a human figure in the lane. It was my mother, her dark green shawl drawn up close around her head. She spoke to me in a voice as plain as if she was standing next to me, and she told me that Dr Farthingale could give me the answer to my question. I knew what she meant without knowing how I knew. I woke up in a sweat, I can tell you, but I was sure I held the truth in my hands. And that was why I had to be the one to confront Dr Farthingale, though it didn't work out quite as I intended. I could never have convinced you that I had solved the case in my dreams, Mr Holmes. Even now, I see that you are sceptical."

"I can't dispute you had a dream, Mr Hewitt. I would only say that -" I suspected my friend was about to begin a philosophical discourse on logic and rational thought, but in mid-sentence he seemed to hesitate. "Who am I to say what is possible or impossible in our dreams," he concluded. "You arrived at the correct answer. I underestimated you, I'm afraid, as did Watson. By the by, you managed that trick with the saddle girth neatly. Still, had Watson been watching you as closely as he should –"

This was the moment I had been expecting, worsened because my humiliation was to take place in front of a witness. To my complete surprise, however, Andrew Hewitt bounded from his chair to take up my defence.

"I won't hear a word against Watson!" he proclaimed, shaking a finger at Holmes. "Remember, you told him to protect me, not to keep me his prisoner. How was he to know what was in my mind? Did you do any better yourself, Mr Holmes? Don't forget how easily you were cornered by my father and brothers."

"I allowed myself to be taken," explained Holmes patiently. "By then I had already observed Dr Farthingale's anxiety to return to the village and I knew he was my man. When I saw your family making towards me, I assumed you had betrayed me to your brother and I thought it best to join forces with them and learn what mischief you had planned without me."

Hewitt rocked complacently on his toes. "But they didn't believe you, did they? Who knows what might have happened if Watson hadn't followed you and convinced them that you were telling the truth? Not a word against Watson, please!"

"I accept your point, Mr Hewitt," Holmes said with a chuckle. "I will not chide him for a mistake that was not his fault."

"Good," said Hewitt, resuming his seat. "Now, Mr Holmes, would you please explain how you solved the mystery? How did you suspect Dr Farthingale when for three and a half years it never occurred to any one of us?"

Holmes drew a last mouthful of smoke and threw the end of his cigarette into the grate. "My first suspicion towards Farthingale was alerted when I learned that he was the last living person to have spoken to your mother that night. The police have been known to make too much of such a circumstance, I agree, but if kept in its proper place, it is useful to remember how often a murderer will admit to having seen his victim very near to the time of death, while not, of course, admitting to the crime itself."

"I don't like your calling Dr Hugh a murderer," Hewitt

almost whispered. "He did not mean to kill her."

"The result is indistinguishable," Holmes pointed out, "but I shall be more delicate if you prefer. Your father and brothers could not suspect the doctor, because they refused to accept that your mother was dead. You accepted the fact, but excluded Farthingale from suspicion because you knew him to be at heart a gentle and a timid man. Having no such preconceptions about anyone, I did not rule out the possibility that he might have been involved in your mother's death. Your brother Edward told me of the doctor's infatuation with her, while the fact that you had not told me indicated that you might have been blinded to certain possibilities about him.

"Then too, of course, he had no witnesses to his activities that night between his departure from Primrose Hill and your arrival at his cottage. Among the close circle of family and friends, only the doctor and your brother David had no one to vouch for them. David actually had witnesses in a negative sense, because no one had seen him anywhere than in his room. In a household this size it is difficult to get from one place to another undetected - I have made some experiments here in the evening hours - and it would be nearly impossible to leave David's room and take a horse from the stable without attracting someone's notice. So, while I could not absolutely clear your elder brother, I put him near the bottom of my list, so to speak. But the most telling piece of evidence in the entire case was your mother's late departure from Primrose Hill that evening."

"Late?" echoed Hewitt. "She left at quarter past seven."

"Exactly," said Holmes. "You said that you expected to see her at the dinner hour of eight. In fact, she ought to have been home sooner if she expected to change her clothing beforehand. It is four miles from Primrose Hill along a winding road overgrown with trees. In the dark, with such moonlight as may have filtered through the branches, it would take the better part of an hour to make the journey - possibly a little longer, for safety's sake. Allowing half an hour to dress, your mother should have left there no later than six-thirty. Why did she stay?"

Hewitt nodded excitedly. "Dr Farthingale's own

account tells us that he waited as long as he could without arousing comment. My mother was trying to avoid him and so she tried to out-wait him. Yes, it is easy to comprehend now, but it was clever of you to see the meaning in it without knowing the full story. None of us gave any thought to the time she left; we just assumed she got talking to Mrs Dudley and lost track of the hour."

"That might well have been the explanation," admitted Holmes. "The difficulty always is to recognise the significance of trivialities without making more of them than is justifiable, given all the facts. The trouble with this case was that there was so little unimpeachable evidence to go on. The police had utterly bungled the physical evidence and the family quarrels made it hard to put together the proper motivation of the participants. It was not until I got what I recognised to be the truth from you, Mr Hewitt, that I felt that I had any firm ground to stand on anywhere. Once I felt absolutely certain that you had not killed your mother –"

"I?" Hewitt shot up in his chair.

"Why not you? When I first arrived I knew nothing of you save that you had a wife who loved you very much. And remember, you were not even willing to admit to your marriage when Watson and I were first introduced to the case. However, I sounded you out in various ways. I baited you to test the violence of your temper, for example, and found that, while you are fairly hot-headed, you would not strike a man whose guard was down. That was in your favour. And then there were those excellent paintings of yours. Still, I was not completely convinced until I had heard your account of the night your mother disappeared. I knew then that you were innocent and that you did not know who was culpable. That knowledge enabled me to narrow the focus of my experiment a great deal. For example, Dr Farthingale's eagerness to be in charge of your care after your injury takes on added significance if one knows you were completely innocent of any knowledge of your mother's fate."

"What do you mean?" asked Hewitt.

"Obviously he wanted you near him in order to learn if he had anything to fear from you. He could not know what you might have seen that night. Remember, when you stood in his parlour, you were only a few scant yards from your mother's body. It is fortunate that you remembered nothing that would incriminate him - how easy it would have been for him to finish you off and claim that you had succumbed to your injuries."

"He would never have been capable of such a thing," Hewitt stated.

"He was capable of keeping you disorientated with drugs for a considerable time, was he not? Did that ever cross your mind?" asked Holmes.

Hewitt dismissed the accusation with a wave of the hand. "If you were so sure it was Dr Hugh, why did you arrange all that subterfuge at the hunt?"

"Watson will tell you," said Holmes, "that I was anything but sure. I needed the proof that can only be obtained by catching the criminal in the act of some further mischief, or else even absolute certainty on my part would be meaningless. I allowed you to suppose that I was more certain than I was, so that your manner would cause alarm to the guilty party. I knew that you were likely to confide in your brother Edward and your friend the doctor. I believed that, if the guilt lay within your family, then Edward was part of the conspiracy, if not in committing the crime, then in its concealment. As it happens he was part of a plan of concealment, although not in the sense that I supposed."

"I accept that you would have handled matters neatly without my cutting off like that. You see why I would have been hopeless as a soldier; I simply cannot do as I'm told."

"What is so dangerous about it, Hewitt," said Sherlock Holmes solemnly, "is that you don't give a man any warning. You say one thing and do the opposite."

Hewitt looked mischievously from me to Holmes and said, "I see from Mr Holmes' face that he was just thinking that should you ever resign from the post of his helper, Watson, I am the last man on earth he would approach to be your replacement."

"I trust Watson has no immediate plans to resign," offered my friend with an arch of his brow.

"None whatsoever," I assured him, settling back into my pillows.

Hewitt laughed merrily. "You will allow Watson to stay here to recover, won't you? I could not bear his being jostled in a railway compartment in his state. Of course, you are both welcome to stay here for as long as you like."

"By all means Watson shall stay and follow when he feels fit," answered Holmes, "but I shall return to London tomorrow. I have other work that demands my attention. I interrupted a fascinating scientific study to take up this case and I would like to resume it as soon as possible."

"I won't argue," said Hewitt gracefully. "And now I shall leave you both in peace and quiet. Looking at Watson has made me realise how much I would appreciate some sleep myself. Until supper then, Mr Holmes, cousin John."

"Hewitt," I called as he turned to go, "hadn't you better stop addressing me as if I were your wife's relative."

"I suppose I had," he paused with his hand on the door knob, "but which of us will tell my father of the deception?" Without waiting for an answer, he darted out of the door.

"An impossible fellow," laughed Holmes with a shake of his head.

"It was very kind of you not to argue with him over his dream. It means a great deal to him to believe he has had some contact with his mother, though I'm sure it sounds fantastic to you."

Holmes pursed his lips and said, "Not entirely fantastic, Watson."

"You don't mean that you subscribe to a belief in supernatural phenomena?" I asked.

"Of course not," he replied crossly, "but I have sometimes gone to sleep with my mind on a problem and found the solution, or the means to the solution, in a dream. Hewitt's more emotional nature merely insists on personifying the thought process into the form of someone he loves. The process itself is identical, however. Have you never experienced it?"

"Well, possibly," I allowed.

"I do not believe the human mind is ever completely unconscious," Holmes went on. "That part which seems to sleep while we are awake wakes when we sleep. Who knows what details of the fatal night were buried at random in Hewitt's illogical brain? What had he observed and forgotten? A second set of wheel tracks on the road? A coating of mud upon the doctor's boot? A dampness on the harness of the doctor's horse? A remembrance of his mother's perfume at the doctor's cottage?"

"Whatever he remembered," I said, "he did because of you."

"Yes, yes," agreed Holmes without enthusiasm. "Still, I am not happy with this investigation even now, Watson. All that I have been able to do is to secure a proper resting place for Elizabeth Hewitt. I wish that I could have done more for her."

"But you have," I exclaimed. "Her good name has been restored. And wouldn't she be pleased that her husband and her youngest son are on good terms now? Holmes, not even you can bring the dead back to life. You must be content that you have solved a mystery with virtually no concrete evidence after three years have passed."

"I shudder to consider how near I came to botching the job," Holmes mused. "I should have been better prepared for Hewitt's impulsive nature. I completely misread the signs in his behaviour yesterday. Had the old doctor been an unrepentant killer, our foolish client would have joined his mother in the northeast corner of the basement, and you and I would have been in some difficulty trying to explain our conduct to the hot-tempered old colonel, make no mistake. We ought to have tied Andrew Hewitt to his saddle."

"I fear that he might still have been able to show me his heels," I admitted. "There is no comparing his horsemanship with mine."

"Your determination compensates for any lack of skill, Watson. You did well."

"I did what I could," I replied calmly, but my heart was glowing. Holmes does not award such garlands of praise lightly, and it was good to know that my efforts had not gone unappreciated. "By the way, Holmes, did you hear any news of the hunt that we missed?"

"It was a blank day. There was such confusion when the Hewitts retired *en masse* that the Master never quite recovered his composure. There were a few sightings, but no kills."

My friend sauntered over to the window and gazed out, his face in repose.

"You seem rather pleased," I remarked.

Sherlock Holmes looked at me over his shoulder. "I am," he said. "It seems to me that there are more pressing evils for man to pursue than a four-footed creature who only behaves in the way that nature intended. I prefer to hunt more dangerous game than that."